# The Terror at Camp Lakeview

## Jordan Steele

# Contents

# 1

## CHAPTER 1

I was running and I couldn't stop. If I did I would be dead right now. I wanted to go back for him but he made me promise not to. I really didn't want to leave him and I hope he's okay. "La'Rayna whatever you do don't stop running." "What about you." "Don't worry about me just keep running?" But S..." "Just keep running I'll be okay promise me you will keep running." "I promise." That was the last thing that he said to me. "Uhhh." I heard screaming I hope that wasn't him. I dived right behind a bush when I heard someone rustling in the woods. I peeked out to see if anyone was there but not too much because I didn't want him or her to see me. I wasn't stupid and I wasn't going to call out and ask who was there. I started to shake and I didn't know if it was because it was freezing cold out or if it was because how scared I am. I wonder if everyone at camp is okay. Well for the people that are still alive. I tried to shake the image of my best friend being murder. But I couldn't it was still playing in my head over and over reminding me that I could be next. It was my fault that she's dead now. She was trying to save me.

When we were running from the camp I feel in a hole in the wood of our cabin and my foot got caught. We heard someone screaming at first but we thought it was just because of the ghost stories. People are always getting scared of the stories because some of them are to be true. But that scream was different it was as if someone was dying. Little did we know it was? We looked out the window and seem something coming out the cabin across from ours and something spotted us. We started to run toward the back of the cabin and sneak out the back way. "Danielle help me my foot stuck." She rushed back over to pull my foot out. Then the door slammed open and there it was standing there. "Come on La'Rayna pull harder." "I'm trying." I finally got my foot unstuck and we headed towards the back door but it wouldn't open. "La'Rayna climbed through the whole." "But D..." I didn't want to leave her and she knew it but it was the only way. "Just do it you're the smallest you will fit and then I'll go it will be faster that way." I did as she said and reached my hand in to help her out. As she grabbed on to my hand that's when it grabbed onto her. "Uhhh let me go." "Danielle I got you don't let go," I said pulling her harder. "Please let go." She looked at me with pleading eyes and that's when I knew she wasn't talking about it and begging him to let her go she was talking to me. I shook my head at her. "No Danielle I got you I will not let you go." I knew I wasn't strong enough but I just couldn't leave her there she didn't leave me.

She looked at me one last time his grip was too strong and I lost hold of her. "Uhhhh." "DANIELLE NOOOOO!" I shouted. How could I let her go? I lie there and watch as he smiled at her then me like this was some kind of game that he was getting ready to play and enjoy because he won. She screamed trying to kick it off her. "Danielle I'm coming" I said while I tried to wiggle my way back in. "No run don't worry about me." She continues to kick until it stabbed her in her stomach. He did it over and over again while she screamed at the top of her lungs and all I could do is sit there and watch. There was so much blood everywhere. I was helpless she was helpless and I couldn't even help her. I was in shock I couldn't move. "Ahhhhh no Danielle...Don't let go...I won't let go...I woke up screaming with Shawn trying to soothe me brushing my hair out of my face. It was only a dream. 'It's okay La'Rayna it was only a dream...shhh it's going to be okay." He said to me. But the sad part about it all was it wasn't just a dream it was a memory that I could never forget. "I'm sorry Danielle." Just the way I said while I hid in the bush over and over as he rocked me back to sleep. "I'm sorry Danielle." "I'm sorry Danielle." "I'm sorry Danielle." "I'm sorry Danielle."

**2**

— • —

## Chapter 2

I was down stairs cooking breakfast when I felt someone's arms wrap around me so I jumped. "Its me." "I'm sorry its just." "I know" He said cutting me off. I still can't shake the feeling of someone else putting their arms on me and the nightmares don't help. Someone coughed which made me and Shawn jumped as he quickly unwrapped his arms from me. "Hey Mrs. Bleu." Hi Shawn" She said dry while eying him. My mother loves Shawn but she loves messing with him more. "Why are you looking at me that Mrs. Bleu?" "Why are you hanging on my daughter like that?" "Aw okay you know me and La'Rayna are just friends." "Umm better be." I love the way my mom picks with Shawn. I fixed my mom plate then fixed me one and sat down. "Oh so I don't get any." "I didn't know if you were hungry." "What you mean you didn't know if I was hungry I just got up just like you...see both of yall be playing games." He said getting up to fix him a plate pointing to my mom and me.

"So Shawn how is the camp coming along" My mother said. I can tell she was trying to be funny but I didn't have a clue what she was talking about. Shawn didn't tell me anything about a camp. "Camp what camp?" I said asking Shawn with a confused tone. "Uhh I got to go to work," He said looking up from the stove puzzled. "I thought you were going to eat first." "Yeah but I'm not that hungry I can wait until lunch." "No you can't skip breakfast that's the most important meal of the day if you don't how will you be able to function at work." "Nah I'll be okay Mrs. Bleu." "I don't think your father would want you to go to work without eating first." "What camp are you talking about." "I have to..." "Answer the question Shawn Taylor Weiss." "Camp Lakeview" He mumbled. "What?" "Camp Lakeview." He mumbled again. "I can't hear you." "Camp Lakeview" He said while turning away from me.

I was lost and confused. I just sat there blank and emotionless. The words Camp Lakeview echo in my head as I went back in time. I was on the bus on the way to camp along with my friend, having a good time with some other kids on the bus until some kid came to the back of the bus starting trouble. "Is this y'all's first time going to this camp." "Yeah...I really never been to a camp before" I said. The reason for that is because back home we had kids camp but it wasn't a real camp. We would just go for half the day play games then go home Monday through Thursday. "Thought so I never seen you on this bus before." He looked us up and down "Well your really going to enjoy this one...if you live." "Wait what do you mean if we live?" "Oh so you guys haven't heard the story about cabin six." We shook our heads no. "Well along time ago at camp Lakeview it was this guy...well they say it's a guy no one really knows what it is." "So what" Shawn said. "The thing is a killer." "Yeah okay" "I'm not lying everyone knows this story." He turned to the other kids on the bus who we were talking to and they shook their heads. "Well cabin six is abandon and it is said to live inside of there...It comes out during the day sneaking around watching kids to see what it wants to kill...after he picks the person he wants to kill he comes back out at night after the camp fires kills them then roast them on the camp fire." "Roast them." "Yeah roast them then take them back to cabin six and eats them....but that's if your lucky...there are many to he things that he does to the campers to scary to even say and some say it happens every year."

Everybody was shocked and scared like they never heard the story before. I was pretty scared myself. "So you came here before." Shawn asked. "Yeah." "Did you ever see anything?" "No but my friend in the other cabin did...I just hope yall know what you guys are getting into." He said with an evil laugh. "Why are you trying to scare everybody?" "I'm not its true." "Well if it's true how come you didn't see anything." "If you don't believe me just see for yourself." He walked off laughing again.

I don't know what was up with that guy. My name is La'Rayna Bleu. I am 12 years old and my so-called mother...I say so-called because she is sending me to camp. Camps are for people who are geeks in my opinion...people who have nothing else to do any the summer because they have no friends so they send them to camp to make friends. Its a good thing my best friend Danielle who is not on the bus because her parents didn't want her on a dirty bus with a bunch of dirty kids they're words not mines. Also my other friend Shawn is coming with me. You know he is a true best friend because I asked him to go with me just one time and he said yes. If I was him I would have said no, if ands, buts about it. Don't ask me again because I'm not going even if you paid me. But that's why I love my Shawn he would do anything for me. As for Danielle going to camp her parents sent her there because she got into trouble and they thought camp was the perfect punishment. "Shawn do you believe that boy." "No he's just trying to scare us." "Are you scared?" "No calm down there's nothing out here and besides why would they keep the camp opened if that stuff did happened." "Your right nothing is going to happen." I hope not.

"Danielle you are crazy." "Hey somebody has to teach that little boy a lesson. He's always picking on someone." "Yeah like on the bus he was telling us this story about this guy who kills and eats the kids at the camp." "What?" "Yeah that's what he said and all the other kids agreed with him but Shawn said he was just trying to scare us." "Yeah maybe because were the new kids." "Right" I said but I still couldn't get over it. It could be the fact that I watch too many horror movies. "Are you guys talking about that things?" Some girl that was in our same cabin spoke up. She looked a little pale and it stood out even more because of her red curly hair, which were in two pigtails and the freckles on her face. "What thing" Danielle said. "Well it's this thing...nobody really knows what it is but it's supposed to go around every year this time and kill the campers." "And you believe that?" said Danielle. "Well yes its true it was all over the news and in the newspapers." "I didn't hear anything about this." "It was only in this town. I live here about 10 miles from the camp." "Well if its true then why do they keep the camp running." I said trying to remember what Shawn told me. It just can't be true if they keep the camp running.

A bunch of kids missing from camp every year just doesn't make sense. "It doesn't happen every year like they say...Well I don't think it does...A few years back the thing started terror on the camp...it first started off as a sick joke...just some kids messing around until one of them went missing." "What happened?" I asked anxious and scared. "No one ever found him." "Okay this doesn't explain anything some kids were messing around and then one went missing." Danielle said doing air quotes when she said missing. "Big deal just some small town talk because you guys have nothing better to do." "It is not." "Well when I see it I will believe it." "Believe what?" Another girl said as she walked in. She was really pretty but it looked like she didn't care. Her clothes were ragged, her hair was in a messy bun, and she looks like she doesn't get much sleep. "Nothing Melly." "Don't call me that I told you never to call me that." "Sorry." "My name is Melissa you got that...that goes for you two as well." She walked over to my bunk and put her army like bag on my bed. "Excuse me but this is my bed." "Excuse me but this is my bed" she said pointing to the name written on the side Melissa C. Wytte. "Sorry." I don't know why I was apologizing she was the one that was rude but I didn't want to hear anything else from her. I grabbed my suitcase and moved to a bonk closer to Danielle. "Come La'Rayna lets go look around camp. Do you want to come um?" "Suzanne Heather Mills but everyone calls me Susie H. "Susie H. would you like to come?" "Oh yes I could show you around."

Once we got outside of the camp I just had to know what was up with that girl. "Whats up with Miss. Melissa C. Wytte." "Oh she's always like that especially since her brother gone missing." I stopped dead in my tracks. "Wait are you saying her brother is the boy that alleged went missing." "Yes, but not alleged is, did go missing."

# 3

## CHAPTER 3

**"S**hawn how could you do this." "La'Rayna it will be good for the camp." "After all that happened there." "That was almost 15 years ago." "Whats that's supposed to mean." "We need to move on we can't be stuck in the past for the rest of our lives." "Stuck in the past are you serious?" "La'Rayna." "No Shawn I live it everyday I will never get over it. We were almost killed out there. I watched my best friend being murder and you are telling me that we need to move on and stop living in the past. I can't even sleep through the night because I keep living it over and over in my dreams." I couldn't even talk to him anymore. I had to get away from him. "La'Rayna wait." Shawn said grabbing my arm. "I'm sorry its...its just that my dad brought the camp and he wants me to run it. He thinks this would be good for everyone you know turn the camp into something positive again...to remember everyone." I looked up at him. "To remember everyone." He shook his head yes. "I want you to help me." I pulled out of his grip. "I can't." 'But." "But nothing I'm not going back there." With that being said I walked out. Him and his father must be crazy. I will never step foot on those campgrounds again. Sometimes I feel like I never left. As if I keep living it over.

"So Susie H. if I mean since her brother went missing why do they keep the camp open matter of fact why would her parents send her back here." "It was a few years ago Melissa was 8 when it happened and her brother was 12. The reason why is because he supposedly went missing at home and not at camp. They say some child molester took him but the police never found his body. Some say her brother is the one killing everybody that's why there's no body. Its also said that the camp paid her parents to keep quite so it can stay open and that's where the whole the killer is her brother thing started. Reason being she keeps coming to the camp and nothing happens to her. "Well has there been any killing since her brother." "Yes, only a few times after other times kids have only been injured and the camp blames it on people not being careful." "None of this is making any sense," said Danielle. "Yeah it never does.

So this is the McKinley hall this is where breakfast, lunch, and dinner is served." I had to get out of here. I tried listing to Shad and Danielle but all of this is too crazy. Maybe they're just trying to scare us because we are new. Yeah that has to be the reason, like some sort of new campers prank. "Susie H. is there a phone out here....you know so we cam call out parents in case of an emergency or if we miss them yeah stuff like that." I said trying not to sound too scared. "No can't get phone service out here. They only way to contact our parents is by letter once a week we are allowed to send letters. Don't worry La'Rayna there just stories." "But you said they were true." "Yeah but that sort of stuff hasn't happen in like forever or "every year." She said doing air quotes. "The only big killing happened almost five years ago you guys will be fine I mean I come here all the time." Yeah sure easy for her to say.

I felt some hands grab onto my leg. I tried to run but then I fell on the ground. As I sat up on the ground I heard some laughing. "La'Rayna are you okay," Danielle said while helping me up. While I was dusting the dirt off of me Shawn and three boys cam from around the corner laughing. "That wasn't funny. "You should've seen the look on your face when you hit the ground." I punched Shawn in the chest as hard as I could. "Ow man what was that for." "For grabbing." "I'm not the one that grabbed you but it was funny." I hit him again. "That's for laughing." "I'm sorry." I looked at who he was with two boys I didn't know and the boy that was on the bus. "Whatever." I turned to walk away with Susie and Danielle. "La'Rayna I said I was sorry." "Why are you with him," I said pointing at the boy on the bus. Shawn turned around and looked. "Who Kirk?" "Oh I didn't know you two were so close." "He is in the same bunk as me. You know he's pretty cool once you get to know him. Let me introduce you them.

We walked over to where they were standing. I was still mad and on top of that my best friend is hanging out with someone that I can't stand. "This is Josh and Kyle and well you already know Kirk." I didn't say anything so Danielle spoke. "Hi my name is Danielle and this is La'Rayna. Um oh and Susie H." "Yes, we know Susie H everyone knows Susie H. They all said at once. "Ha ha very funny guys." "Its not our fault you have to make yourself known to everyone at the camp," said Josh "I do not." "Come on guys we have to meet in the Bailey Hall," Kirk said. "For what," I said with sort of an attitude I was still mad at them. "A meeting with all the campers and camp counselors. Be prepared to be bored its nothing but rules, rules, and more rules." We were in the Bailey Hall sitting there listening to all of the rules and how "fun" camp was going to be.

Boy these counselors were lame and corny. I was sitting next to Kirk the last person I wanted t sit next to but he wasn't that bad. He was pretty funny. He kept on mocking the camp counselors. After the rules and getting to know the other kids in the camp it was time for dinner. We headed back to the McKinley Hall.

**4**

**CHAPTER 4**

It was kind of hard sleeping the first night. I still couldn't shake the feeling there was a killer around here somewhere. I felt like someone was watching me. I woke up and there Melissa was sitting there glaring at me. When I looked up she turned her head and acted like she wasn't looking at me. I don't know what that girl problem is. I got up and shook Danielle. "Can people get their beauty sleep here." "Like that would help you." Melissa said across the room. "And you need it more than anyone in here." Danielle snapped back. Melissa rolled her eyes and walked into the bathroom. "I can't stand her. I got an idea." Danielle said still looking at the bathroom. "What is it." "Shh just come on." We got up and walked into the bathroom. We heard the shower running that only meant one thing Melissa was in the shower. Danielle turned to me and said "Okay you take those two toilets and I'll take these two." "Got it." I walked into the first stall and flushed the toilet and I could hear that Danielle did the same thing. "Ahhhh." We heard Melissa scream as me and Danielle ran out the bathroom laughing so hard. Here in these bathrooms when you flush the toilet the water gets hot but little did we know when you flush the toilets at the same time all of the water backs up and goes into the shower. Double laugher for us. Melissa comes out with blue stuff all over her making Danielle and I laugh even harder. "Have a nice shower." "You two messed with the wrong one." Danielle got up and stood in Melissa face." "No you messed with the wrong one oh and you might want to take a shower before you kill a skunk wouldn't want to harm your cousin now would you." Danielle is too crazy she's always pulling stuff like this on people who say or do something to her. Like yesterday when we heard Kirk trying to scare some other kids.

"Hey you what do you think you're doing?" "Just enlighten the campers on their stay here for the next few weeks whats it to you?" "Oh so you want to get smart." "I don't need to get smart but I must seem like a genius to an idiot like you." Kirk turned back around to the crowd. So she ties his shoes together and pulled down his pants. Everyone pointed and laughed at him but when he tried to turn and walk away he fell flat on his face. "That will teach you." We walked to our cabin. "Danielle you are crazy." "Hey somebody has to teach that little boy a lesson. He's always picking on someone." "Yeah like on the bus he was telling us this story about this guy who kills and eats the kids at the camp." "What?" "Yeah that's what he said and all the other kids agreed with him but Shawn said he was just trying to scare us." "Yeah maybe because were the new kids." "Right" Right are still my exact thoughts.

Maybe all of this stuff is just some crazy made up story by Melissa trying to get attention off of her brothers disappearance. I did notice yesterday at dinner that she was getting treated better than everyone else. "Are you guys ready?" Susie H said walking into the cabin. Now where did she go early this morning? I didn't even notice she was missing. There's something strange about that girl, she's a little off at times. And she's always a little too happy then most even to be at a camp where there are "killers" on the loose. When I think about it I wouldn't be surprised if she was the killer. But then again her face was drain of color when she was telling us the story. "Yes we are ready what are we doing today?" I asked. Yes we are ready all of that thinking I was getting ready. I just don't wake up and go. Just so you don't get the wrong idea. "We are going canoeing today. You guys are pretty lucky this year is the first time that we have canoeing on the first day." "I didn't get dressed for canoeing." "You will be fine in that but first up is he little stuff like basketball, arts and craft, dance class, archery, then canoeing." "All of that." "Yes just the intro for some classes. Its like that all week so for the rest of the summer we can go to whatever, go to whatever site as we please some classes on certain days though. Now lets hurry we have to go, go, go, go. "Ok ok don't get your panties in a bunch Susie its not like you are the camp counselor or something," Melissa said. That was the first time I heard Melissa sound kind of nice.

We went down to the McKinley hall to have breakfast first. We got out breakfast and went over to sit next to Shawn and the rest of the guys in his cabin. Melissa went to go sit with the privilege kids at the camp her being the most privileged of them all. "Are you guys ready for the into classes today." Danielle. "Yeah looking forward to being bored to death," said Kirk. "What do you guys have first," Shawn asked me. "We have basketball first. "Oh." "Why what do you have first." "All of the boys cabins go backwards from the girls so we have archery, dance class, arts and craft, basketball then canoeing." "We have canoeing last too." "Yeah but we might not be in the same group. They do this every year even though they split us up we still have groups that are synched together at the same time. So what you girls are in cabin 5 so your group will be group 1-4 of all girls. We are in cabin 10 so we will be in group 10-15 but they switch up the boys and girls so that doesn't mean at the end we will meet the girls cabin 10-12," Kirk said filling us in. I hope we meet up today the point of Shawn coming to camp was for me. "Don't worry even if we don't see each other after this week is over we can go to any site we want."

The intro classes are kind of boring just like Kirk said they would be so I don't want to bore you guys to death with that. We had to go in groups by the number on our cabins like 1-4. And since the boys cabins are in-between the consolers we wouldn't be meeting up until the end. All it was blah blah the rules. Like do we really need rules in arts and crafts? Rule number one paint on the paper and not the table what are we in pre-school? We did have some rules for the harder things in there like what to do with pottery and stuff. This instructor was pretty cool he let us do a little some on the first day even though we weren't supposed to. He said rules are for people who have no guidance's that is not already built in. I don't know what that means I think he's some type of hippie guy but if he's not going to bore us wit a bunch of rules I'm cool with that.

Finally we made it to canoeing where we would meet up with some of the guys at camp. I hope we meet up with Shawn. Just as I thought that. "Having fun." "Tons I really enjoyed the into to basketball I never knew what a basketball was until hat class." Shawn laughed and we got yells at by the instructor. He snapped his neck at us fast and said. "Now pay attention we don't need none of you coming up to me asking a bunch of question that I already answered. I hate answering question I already answered." "Well if you taught this last year isn't that the same thing." I said all innocent. I was being smart on purpose because he called us out for no reason her didn't even start yet. He walked over to us and stood in front of me. He looked me up and down then smirked at me. "Well you're right so how about you tell us the safety of canoeing." I was trying to think of something really cleaver to come back at him but right when I did he said, "I didn't think so. Your on my list."

He walked back over to where he was standing and started to explain. "I'm on his list well there's something he just doesn't know he just made the himself the first person of my list who the killer might be at this camp. Well I think there are three people that could be the killer consoler Cutlip, Melissa and then there's Susie H. I really have to get these thoughts out my head and start trying to have some fun but its kind of hard. It may or may not be true. I felt someone staring at me so I look up and Melissa was staring at me through the crowed of people. She turned her head a little like she was looking at me. Its funny I still feel someone staring at me. I look all around but no one.

**5**

**CHAPTER 5**

"La'Rayna are you okay," Shawn asked. "Yeah I'm fine." "You just seem a bit nervous." "She must still be scared about those stories people been telling." "I am not." "Yeah if you say so." "I'm not I just never been in a boat before," I said lying. well more like half lie. Someone is watching me and its freaking me out and I never been in a boat. "It will be fine you can be my partner." We were going canoeing. The camp staff were telling us the rules like two to a canoe, keep life jackets on at all times, and no going pass the yellow ropes and other safety stuff. To be honest I was still a little shake up about those stories but the people around here walk around like its nothing. Maybe I'm just worrying for nothing. "Shawn." I whispered. "Yeah." "Do you feel like someone is watching us?" "No, La'Rayna you are worrying too much." "But." "But those are just stories try to have fun while we're here for the next three months." "Ok ."

He was right we are going to be here for three months and acting paranoid isn't going to help. Besides the feeling that someone was watching us faded away as soon as I clam down.

I have just been overreacting and I need to start having fun before I ruin everyone's trip. I was in the canoe with Shawn we were pretty far out and Kirk, Danielle, and Susie wasn't pretty far behind with a few selected other kids at the camp. Most of everyone stayed pretty close to the shore. "Shawn lets go in some." "Why?" "You know I hate deep water." "You're wearing a life jacket and besides I wouldn't let you fall out." "Isn't this great," Kirk said canoeing over to us. "Yeah really great." He is cool and all but he's a very combative like he has to prove he's the best or something. "Whoa whoa." "Kirk stop playing before we fall in." "I'm just joking." "Well sit down were not supposed to be standing up in the canoe." "What could happen?" "Either you sit willing or by force you choose." Danielle is crazy. "Alright don't get your panties in a bunch." As he was starting to sit down he tripped on the paddle and fell in the water. "Oh my gosh Kirk." We all yelled. "Kirk." We were searching in the water for him but no sign. Our boat started to rock. "Shawn," I screamed. "Don't worry." Then it stopped. "Kirk." We were all looking on the same side so we didn't see this coming. "Boo." We all jumped back. "Aw Kirk your such a jerk." "I was just fooling." He said laughing. "Well it wasn't funny." "Lighten up." He climbed back in the canoe and we all went back to shore. "Why are you all wet McCray?" "Well uhh." "His paddle fell in the water and I tried to push it back to him with mine paddle so the water splashed him. " "Yeah that's what happened." "Why aren't you wet?," Cutlip said eying Danielle. "I moved out the way," she said. "Next time keep your paddle inside the boat." That was a close one we all could've been banned from canoeing for Kirk little stunt. It's just like Shawn though he is always covering for someone or helping someone out. Its been a long boring day and I just want to eat, go to bed, and hope tomorrow is going to be better. Day two of rules can't come fast enough.

I've been running for quite sometime trying to get away from...uh I'm not too sure what or whom I'm running from. The last thing I remember was being in the equipment room. Consoler Cutlip told me to put the bag of balls in there after a game of dodge ball or what he likes to call it a game to toughen up weak little men. It was so dark in there and there wasn't a light switch to turn on so I couldn't see. I went to the back looking for a place to put the bag of balls in. I heard a loud crashing sound like glass breaking then someone shouted. I went to go see what happened but nothing. I look and turn around and seen a shadow and a growling noise letting me know that was my que to get up on out of there. I'm no dummy I watch too many scary movies to just stand there or going to look for what was making that sound. Besides I'm black we always go first. I ran outside and into Jake. "Jake do not go in there." "Uh what, why?" "There's something in there no you can't go in there." "Its fine there's nothing out here besides consoler Cutlip told me to put the bag of balls inside there." "What?" I had this confused look on my face. How could he be putting the bag of balls up if that's what I was doing? I looked down into his hand and seen a bag of balls. I heard him laugh so I look up and Jake had this evil look in his eye and started to grin. His laugh got even louder and he opened up the bag of balls expect there wasn't any balls in there but... "No." I shouted while shaking my head then took off running towards the woods. I had to stop for a breather. I leaned up against a tree for a while I hope everyone at the camp is ok. I just realized its Jake he's the killer. 'Crack' 'Crack' I heard a noise so I started to back up and bummed into someone. "Ahh." "Clam down its me. "Shawn oh man I glad I found you." "What are you doing way out here?" "I was putting the balls up in the equipment room like Mr. Cutlip told me to but then I heard a scream and glass breaking so I went to go check it out but nothing was there and then there was a shadow so I ran and Jake...Oh my gosh Jake he is the killer." I said panting and speaking really fast. "What Jake a killer?" "Yes." "Come on," Shawn said pulling on me sleeves toward the camp. "No we can't go back." "And why not." "I just told you." Wait why was Shawn out here. "A killer La'Rayna there is no killer out here." "What are you doing out here." "I was coming back from the fishing site." "The fishing site is that way. I said point in the op piste direction from the cameo site. And, and you came from that direction." "So I got lost." "No, no, no." I turn and ran. "La'Rayna wait. La'Rayna." I heard Shawn calling my name but no way was I going back. I kept running until I tripped and fell and Shawn caught up to me. "La'Rayna what is going on," He said trying to help me up. "Let me go you're all apart of it." "Apart of what?" My eyes grew wide. "La'Rayna whats wrong." "Shawn behind you look out." It was too late his head was lying right next to me and I was covered in blood. I knew I was next. "Ahh."

I woke up sweating. It was just a dream. "La'Rayna are you ok," Danielle said. "Yes I'm fine just a bad dream." "Must of been some dream you were tossing around for a while," Susie H said. "No it was nothing." "Are you sure because if you wanted to talk about it I'm here?" "Danielle I'm fine sorry I woke everyone up." "But." I cut her off before she could say anything else. "No really its okay," I said flashing a fake smile so she wouldn't worry. "Go back to bed. Both Danielle and Susie H got back into bed and went to sleep. I looked across the room Melissa was siting there staring at me she smirked and laid back down and went to sleep. As for me I faked like I was sleep for the rest of the night. Who was I fooling I was too scared to go back to sleep again. So all I could do was try to figure out what that dreamed meant. Wait who's Jake?

**6**

CHAPTER 6

"La'Rayna. " "Yeah I'm fine." "Uh that's nice but I didn't ask that. But speaking of you being okay are you sure because you have this crazy look in your eye." Shawn made this funny face. I laughed at him. "I do not look like that." "I know it was more like this," He said making another face. "Um Shawn do you know anyone name Jake." "No why?" "It was just a dream that I had that I'm trying to figure out." "It was just a dream." "I know Shawn but this dream was so real." "Look La'Rayna you have to get over those stories I didn't come here with you so you can freak out over nothing. If this all you are going to do then I don't want to hang around you I want to at least have fun if I'm going to be here for two months." Shawn walked off and went over to where Kirk and them were. I guess I was ruining everyone's vacation but something just wasn't sitting right with me. I couldn't let this feeling go. Maybe I am taking this over board Danielle is mad at me now Shawn is mad at. I felt some behind me and I turned around really quick. "What did I scare you?" Melissa said. I didn't respond. "What cat gots your tongue or something I see I of your friends have left." "So what it to you." "Oh so your trying to be the bold one now aren't you now that your friends what's her name isn't here." "You don't scare me." "I don't do I. You should be scared." "Hey is there a problem here?" Ms. Kanto one of the camp consolers said coming towards us as everyone turned to face us. "No there isn't a problem Ms. Kanto." Melissa said smirking. I wanted to wipe that smirk off her face so bad but I knew that would get me in trouble maybe even sent home. "Good now you both go separate ways I don't want to hear anymore out of you two for the rest of the day." I really don't understand what is up with these counselors I've been getting in trouble for nothing. I walked in the other direction than Melissa into a group of kids who were playing. "Are you okay?" "Why do you care?" "Look I'm sorry about earlier." "Yeah you should be you didn't even listen to what I was saying." "I know." "I mean my dream could have been about me winning a trip to Disney or something." "I know I'm sorry La'Rayna." "No I'm the one who is sorry I'm ruin everybody chance at having a good time. I promise I will try to be more happy and have fun."

Try and be happy and have fun. Try to be happy and have fun try to be happy and have fun. I remember when I got back from camp people thought I was crazy because all I could say was try to be happy and have fun. I would say it over and over again. Don't ask me I don't know why. I think it was pretty strange for a girl who was almost murder to go around saying try to be happy and have fun. This is really starting to bother me because I keep living the memory of Camp Lakeview everyday. Sometimes it's as if I'm still that little girl at camp. I can't believe Shawn's father why would you open up that camp after what happened there. His son was almost killed out there.

**7**

CHAPTER 7

"Ahhh." "La'Rayna are you okay." "Yeah I'm fine." I said wiping the dirt off of my pants. "I just fell." We were going hiking. Well we weren't supposed to be going hiking but when you hag out with someone like Kirk you end up ding things that your not supposed to do. I only went to prove that I wasn't afraid of getting into trouble. "Your such a scary cat." "I am not." "Are too that's why you don't want to go with us." "Because we can get in trouble." "Aw trouble smouble who cares...besides would I get you into trouble?" "Gee let me guess I just meet you and you already got us into trouble yesterday." "Well this time its going to be different." "Yeah come on La'Rayna it would be fun." "If you say so." So that's how we all ended up here.

"Guys don't you think we should be heading back?" I asked. I really didn't want to keep going. I was afraid we would get lost and I can't see the camp site anymore. "Quit being such a baby we just started. "Well excuse me, I didn't know an hour of walking was just a few minutes. Maybe I should go back to school and learn how to tell time Miss. Cosmos Clock." I said point at my watch. I don't know who invited her anyways. "An hour we couldn't possibly been gone that." Danielle questioned. "Tepee left at two and it's going on three." I lied but how would they know they don't have a watch. "Let me see." I showed Danielle my watch. "Really it doesn't feel like we've been walking or that long." I moved the time up on my watch just so we wouldn't have to go that far. We really only been walking for about 30minutes. "Come on Ray Ray we haven't even made it passed cabin six yet. Once we reach there we are almost at our destination. Kirk chimed in. He knows I hate the name Ray Ray but yet he insist on calling me that. I just glared at him. "Where are we going anyways Kirk?" Shawn asked. "You'll see." "Are we just going to stand here and have a tea party or are we going to get moving." Melissa said with an attitude. I really dislike her.

We took off walking again. Everyone was joking around during the hike, well everyone except Melissa and I. She was just naturally evil and I didn't want to be here in the first place. I was lagging behind everyone else in case we had to run. Believe me I wanted to be the first one out there. I keep getting this strange feeling like we are being followed. Every time I turn around there's nothing there. Shawn must have sensed my uneasiness and stopped the game of kick the can; in our case kick the rock, and came back to chat. I guess anything to pass the time of this long hike. "Hey." "Hey" I said back. "Are you cool?" "Yeah."

"Come up here and playa game with us." "No I'm fine." "Are you sure?" "Yes." "Try to be happy and have fun okay." "I am"

We finally made it to cabin six. "Hey Ray Ray want to go inside cabin six?" Kirk said trying to be funny. "Yeah Ray Ray want to go inside cabin six." "Yeah Ray Ray cabin six." Kirks lackeys Josh and Kyle said. "Like even" I spit back. "Why don't you go since the almighty Kirk that's not afraid of anything." "Because...uh...I've already been in there." "Yeah he's been in there," said Josh. "We all have." "Yeah right." "We have a few years ago didn't we Melissa." Kirk said putting an emphasis on Melissa's name. She just stood there and smirked."Good for you but we didn't come here for this." Danielle said annoyed. "Why are you afraid?" Kirk said. "No it's just some stupid cabin. "Well I dare ya then...I dare all ya to go inside for 30minutes." "Yeah 30minutes if ya can." "Ha if they can I bet they can't." "Danielle rolled her eyes. "Can you two flunkeys stop it." "What about the cave man?" Shawn suggested. Cave what cave. I guess Kirk told Shawn where we were going. "Don't worry man we'll get to that. Just go inside." "Fine come on guys but I'm not staying in there that long we have to get moving." Danielle hissed at them. Shawn and Danielle begin to walk towards cabin six. I just stood there frozen like a block of ice. Who knows what lies in there. "Baby Ray Ray do you need someone to hold your hand?" I got mad all over again he was being his obnoxious self. "Shut up Kirk I'm sick of you mouth. You act like your not afraid of anything but I bet you have never been inside yourself. When I come out and if you can't tell me one thing that's in there in detail you have to spend the night inside the cabin by yourself" I yelled at him. "Um." I turned my nose up at him and rushed passed Danielle and Shawn and stood on the porch to cabin six. I reached for the door knob.okay La'Rayna you can do it. I grabbed the rusty door knob and turned around. "You two coming or not?" Danielle and Shawn soon followed me unto the porch. I turned the knob and opened the door.

As soon as I opened the door bats began to fly out above our heads. I ducked and heard Kirk and the guys screaming. I wasn't afraid of bats because back home during the summer they are always making their way into our attic and I get to help my dad move them outside. I turned around to make sure everyone was okay and seen Melissa just smirking. That girl has some serious issues. I processed to walk until I felt a pair of hands on my shoulder. "Wait." I heard Shawn say. "What is it?" "Let me go first." Shawn the protector. Not that there is anything wrong with that. I'm glad he's willing to go first. Besides the little courage that I managed to muster up is now gone. "Okay." I barley got out in a whisper. I took one large gulp of spit and followed after him...well after him, after Danielle of course.

"Ugh it smells in here." Danielle said covering her nose with her hand while waving her other hand in the air. The smell was awful. You know if you leave meat out for days then throw it in the trash and let it sit until the trash men comes. Well it smells worse than that. But it was dark and eerie. The only light was coming in from the cracked boards on the windows. There was glass shatters everywhere on the floor. Everything was covered in white sheets...well what used to be white sheets on top odd drift and dust. Talk about abandoned thus place was worse than abandon. "I can't believe they just left this place to sit and rot." Rot was the correct word because that's exactly what it looked and smelled like. "Yeah I guess they could've tore it down. Maybe it made for good ghost stories during camp fires" Shawn said. "What ghost stories and for what?" Danielle question. He shrugged. "I don't know maybe to scare kids into being good. We stared to look around. I was getting ready to go over to the used to be closet but then this bright light skinned in my face. I turned to see where it was coming from. It was coming from the used to be dresser. It was exactly like the ones in our cabin expect it was broken down. I walked over to it and part of the top drawer was opened a little. I looked inside and seen thus thing glistening. I opened the drawer a little bit more and reached in and grabbed the piece of mental. It looked like an id bracelet with writing on it that I couldn't make out. "Okay guys lets get out of here I can't handle the smell any longer" Danielle said. Shawn and I shook our heads in agreement and we headed towards the door. I shoved the bracelet in my pocket before anyone noticed it. I felt someone looking at me and I turned behind me. I noticed something in the closet. I tried to look harder but a pair of hands grabbed my hand causing me yo jump and turn around. "What are you looking at?" Shawn asked concern. " Nothing." "Well come on guys this smell is giving me a headache." We walked out.

"So Kirk name one thing and describe in detail what was in there. It shouldn't be so hard since you've been in there" I said. "Well uh." I could see he was looking for the answer. He's never stepped foot in the cabin a day in his life. "Whatcha looking up at the sky for the answers not up there?" I snapped at him. "Uh I know that what does it matter where I look I know what's in there how about a dresser." Of course he could guess that because the cabin is the exact match to all the others just abandon. "You made that up." "I did not." "Whatever." I just rolled my eyes and let it go. "Come on babies time to stop playing house and head to the cave" Melissa said.

We begin the rest of the trek to our destination which I guess was this cave. I don't get why we are going. Like what are we supposed to find there. "OK! This is it guys. We finally made it to caveman's doom. Isn't this cool?" Kirk said. The cave looked like kind of creepy. It has moss and vines growing on the outside and it felt was kind of cool and damped by the entrance. There was a bunch of broken and rotten wood laying all around. Nothing cool about this. "I guess man but why are we here?" Shawn questioned. "To check it out duh man get with it. Nobody knows...where this one goes." "So you expect us to go in there and explore like we are Lewis and Clark?" said

Danielle. "Yeah why come all this way to stand outside quit being a bunch of babies." said Melissa. She was really getting on my nerves. "Look Dora the explorer we already went into cabin six while y'all just stood outside now y'all want us to go into some cave in the middle of the woods that leads to who knows where. How about no and you go have your little sick and twisted strange fun." I said. "Come on guys it will be fun." Kirk said while he came around and stood between me and Danielle and put his arms around our shoulders. I looked over at Shawn. He just shrugged. "It could be fun but you guys go first and don't be pulling any tricks." He said. "Lead the way Dora" Danielle snickered at Melissa. She just rolled her eyes and went in first.

"So Kirk why do they call this caveman's doom." Shawn said. I nudged him with my elbow. He looked at me like what. Always the curious one. Well curiosity killed the cat. I really didn't need to hear the story I already didn't want to go in. "It's called caveman's doomed because of what happened years ago right before cabin six was abandon. And this is the place that the killer is supposed to be hiding out at because this place is for forbidden. "So if the killer is hiding out here why are we in here you big dork?" "Because that's just a story." "So is everything else that you ever told us." "Okay guys I want to know what happened before the whole cabin six." "Anyways back to the story before I was rudely interrupted." I just rolled my eyes at him. "There was this guy once who was hiking in these very woods alone. A big storm came and he couldn't find his way home and he came across this cave for shelters. At least he thought it was shelter. He went in and never came out." "Well why?" Danielle asked cutting him off. "Well maybe if I can get through the story then we will all know. Anymore question before I finish?" "Just get on with already" Shawn said annoyed. "What he didn't know was that there was this thing dealing in the cave nobody knows what it was so don't ask but it had claws and sharp teeth." "Hold up if nobody knows what it was how would you know that it had claws and sharp teeth." again Danielle said cutting him off. "Because now hush." "You hush." "Ugh just let him finish the story." "Okay okay." Danielle and him could go at it forever. "So the thing attacked him and  the flood from the storm swallowed him up. They didn't find him until six months later when Camp Lakeview opened up for the summer." Man Kirk is really bad at telling scary stories. I don't even believe this one. "They even say till this very day that the thing sometimes roams these woods at night looking for his next victim."

OK, now I was really scared because I have been feeling like something has been watching us since we been on the hike. But I'm trying not to show that I'm scared so I got argumenta-tive. "Wait a minute. Which one was it? Did the thing eat him or did he drown?" "Both!" "That's impossible because it doesn't make any sense he was either eaten alive or he drowned. You can't be eaten alive then drown because you will already be dead and vice versa. "Hey I'm just repeating the legend." "Whatever." "Shh did you hear that." Kirk said putting his arms out in front of us." "No." "There it goes again." He started to make scary sounds. Even dumb and dumber Josh and Kyle joined in. "Knock it of guys it's not funny." Shawn said. I can tell he was tried of the stupid tricks. "Yeah quit it" I said. "Shut up guys" said Danielle. "Let's just get out of here I said. I turned and tripped on a rock. "Ouch." "La'Rayna are you okay" Shawn said bending down to me." "No I think I twisted my ankle." Kirk and the guys were still making that sound. "Guys if you don't knock it off I will knock you out" Shawn yelled at them. I have never seen him so mad before he's always so calm and cool. They shut their mouths. "Come on I can't believe you guys were actually scared it was just a joke." "No we weren't scared you moron it was annoying" said Danielle. "Come on help me get La'Rayna up so we can head back to the camp." Shawn said giving directions. I'm glad someone else needs to take charge of what's going on because we all know Kirk can't handle any situation.

We made our way back down to the camp. I definitely twisted my ankle but I could walk on it much better. Shawn didn't allow it anyways. He is do protective especially when it comes to me. When we reach the end of the camp I looked back and stopped thinking something was missing. I turned and looked at thought wheres Melissa?

**8**

CHAPTER 8

I was sitting in the psychiatrist office waiting to go home. I've been coming here since I left Camp Lakeview. I don't know why they continue to force me to come I will never speak. Talking about what happened to a stranger isn't going to help me. "La'Rayna would you like to speak to me on what happened when you were younger?" Dr. Lawson asked. She ask me the same question every time and I say nothing every time. She writes something down on her pad like always and then I sit there until it's time for me to leave. She wasn't my first psychiatrist. I have went through five because they get fed up with me and felt they could no longer help me. My first psychiatrist had it the worst. When we first got back from Camp Lakeview I couldn't trust anybody but Shawn. I was almost put in a psych ward from the way I was acting. They couldn't control me. This lady though she was determined to "help" me.

"When I was younger I went to camp too" she said looking up from her pad. She pulled her glasses from her face and set them on her desk I front of her. I just sat there not giving any type of emotion. Am I supposed to care if this lady went to camp. Does she really think this is going to get me to talk about what happened at Camp Lakeview. "I had a lot of fun we went hiking, canoeing, swimming...um." She put her pad down on her desk. "Told scary ghost stories." I laughed inside my head and just stared at her. This lady must be crazy. We had fun we told scary ghost stories. Telling me you had fun when you went to camp isn't going to help the girl who was almost murder. Telling me you told ghost stories isn't going to get me to tell you want happened. I glanced up at the clock it was almost time to leave. She noticed because her eyes flickered at her wrist. She signed and said that I could leave early if I wanted to. I got up and went outside Shawn was waiting for me in his car.

"Have fun." He joked. I wasn't amused. I glared at him and he laughed. I was still mad at him for not telling me he and his dad was trying to reopen Camp Lakeview. I guess he noticed. "So your still made at me?" "No, Shawn I like the fact that you are trying to reopen camp murder and not tell me." "Look La'Rayna it wasn't my idea and I was against it at first too but when my dad explained what he wanted to do I agreed." "What could you possibly agree to that would make this the best thing to do" I began yelling. I didn't mean to. If you will listen to me and let me explain I'll tell you" He yelled back. I was taken back a little. He has never yelled at me. He pulled the car over on the side of the rode. "La'Rayna look at me." I just kept looking out the window. "La'Rayna please look at me I'm sorry for yelling at you but you won't let me explain." I looked up at him. "I, sorry it's just..." I trailed off and looked down. He grabbed my chin pulled my head up with his hand and made me look at him. "I know I was there." He took a deep breath and began. "My dad is reopening Camp Lakeview because he wants to honor everyone who died there. He's trying to shed some light on the tragedy that occurred there. He has a very solid plan and I'm going to help him. Reopening the camp is going to help us move on and stop morning the loss and to start celebrating their lives. It will be good for all of us. It will help us." "I miss her." He wiped the tears that I didn't even know have fallen from my face. In fact most of the time I don't even know when I'm crying anymore. "I miss her too."

We pulled up to this huge building where Shawn's father works. I haven't been here since we were kids. We would play hide n go seek in the office when his dad had a meeting that we obviously couldn't go in. His dad had this big Ol' black chair that we used to spin each other in. I miss those days. Nothing to worry about. To be a kid again. "Why are we here?" I asked while we walked to the elevator. "I have to pick up some things from my office. When we got back from camp we both had to see a therapist for awhile. Later we got older; Shawn got better went to college and began working for his fathers company. Me however did not. I can't function in reality sometimes so it's hard for me to do anything. Hence why I'm still seeing a psychiatrist. I do remember when I was a little girl I wanted to be doctor so that I could help people. Blood frightens me now. If I cut myself or anything I start to have flash backs. It sucks I know. I'm trying to get better.

We walked into Shawn's office and I heard kids laughing. I turned around and seen three kids; two little girls and a boy shooting water guns at each other. They looked just like us when we were younger. It made me smile. "La'Rayna are you okay?" Shawn asked. I turned back around. "Yes why?" "Because you were smiling into space." "Uh what there was..." I turned back to were the kids were supposed to be but they were gone. "Never mind," I said. He walked behind his desk and grabbed some blueprints. "What are those?" "Blueprints of...um of the camp. Do you want to see?" I shook my head no. "Okay let's go." We were headed out his office until we bumped into his dad." "La'Rayna it's so good to see you how have you've been." "Fine Mr. Weiss." I said moving behind Shawn. Trust issues, I hate it. It's not as bad as it used to be. "Well that's nice to hear. Shawn can I speak with you for a moment?" Shawn turn to look at me. I nodded letting him know it was okay to leave me for a while. He walked back into his office with his dad and closed the door.

"Danielle you can't get me." "I bet I can." "Shawn look out slow poke is coming." I heard laughter. I walked over towards the window in the lobby and peaked out of the curtain. My eyes widen. Those kids again. They looked up at me and waved and smiled. They mouthed to me to come play with them. I know why they looked like us before they are us. I felt a hand grabbed my shoulder so I jumped and turned around. "Sorry, Shawn said. "Don't do that you almost gave me a heart attack. "What are you looking at anyways there's nothing out there." "Nothing." "Are you ready to go?" "Yes."

When we walked in the house my mother was standing at the door. "La'Rayna can I speak to you for a moment." Shawn looked at me. "Well I have some work to do so il let you guys talk." He went upstairs. We walked into the living room and sat down on the couch. I already know where this is going. After all of my sessions with my psychiatrist she always wants to know how they went and if they made a "break" through. "I'm kind of tired of having this talk. But you need to start talking about what's going on with you." I raised my eye brows at her. "La'Rayna why don't you ever talk to your therapist she is there to help you." "I'm tired of talking about this too." I started to get up and walk away. "La'Rayna sit down now!" She yelled at me. Yelling at me doesn't help it only frightens me. I sat down afraid of what might happened. "It's been about 15 years you have to try and move on I want my little girl back." "Your little girl died at Camp Lakeview."

**9**

— • —

## CHAPTER 9

Welcome to Camp Lakeview. The broken wooden sign above my head read. I stood there not believing that I'm actually back at this place. Everything that happened came flooding back into my brain. I've been trying to block it for all these years and it still hasn't gone away. I began scanning the area and flashes of the past crept up in my memory. The place was dark and empty. I don't get how anyone can turn this evil place into something positive. It's just dead like me.

I head laughter but I couldn't pin point where it was coming from. I started to walk around trying to find out who it was. Things started to seem fuzzy and I couldn't see straight. I kept walking until I stood right in front of cabin five. The cabin where Danielle and I stayed. The cabin where I watched my best friend die and I didn't do anything to help save her. I took a deep breath and walked in. I don't know why it was like I couldn't control my body. The place is exactly how I remember it. So strange, nothing was damaged. All of the beds were made nothing out of place. I heard the door creak open then slam shut. It made me jump. I was frightened not sure weather to run or turn around. "Oh, there you are we have been looking all over for you." I heard a familiar voice say which made me turn around. "Dan...Daniel...Danielle?" I questioned. "Yes silly it's me who else would it be? Me and Shawn have been waiting by the lake and you never showed up." She took a step closer to me and I backed up. "Are you okay La'Rayna?" "How can this be your dead." "Dead how could I be dead. Don't be silly come on Shawn is waiting on us." She tried to reach for me but I moved back. "If your not dead then why do you still look like a child?" "What are you talking about?" I pointed towards the mirror. She turned and faced the mirror. I was much taller than her now since I'm now a grown 22 year old and she's still a small 12 year old child. "Oh your right you got old La'Rayna" she said swing back and forth in the mirror. "What happened to you. Why did you leave me?" Blood began covering her clothes. "I didn't mean to." I barley got out. "But you did and you never came back. I waited for you. Why didn't you come back?" "Danielle I'm sorry." Tears began welling up in my eyes. "Well sorry isn't good enough!" She said yelling. She turned to me and her face changed. I screamed and woke up and realized I was on the couch.

Another dream. I started to shake uncontrollably and breath heavy. "La'Rayna are you okay I heard you screaming." Shawn said coming from upstairs. Once he reach me he grabbed onto me and tried to clam me down. "La'Rayna it's okay what's wrong what happened?" "I saw Danielle." "Huh." "She tried to kill me...she tried to kill me Shawn" I said gasping for air. "Calm down try and breath." He slowly ran his fingers through my hair as I laid my head on his chest. I finally calmed down. "Shawn it's my fault." "What are you talking about?" "It's my fault that Danielle is dead." "It's not you fault." "But I left her and she needed me." "La'Rayna if you didn't do what she said you would be dead to. And if you would have died out there I might as well be dead. Danielle saved your life okay. She wanted you to be safe okay." "She told me that she waited for me and I never came back. I told her I was sorry and she said it wasn't good enough." He sat me up and looked in my eyes. "Did you see her just now?" I know what he's talking about. He wants to know if I actually seen her physically standing her. Trying to make sure I'm not going crazy. "I'm not crazy Shawn I was sleep." I snatched away from him. "So it was a dream." "It didn't feel like a dream." I whisper I know he heard me but he let it go. "La'Rayna don't make me have to commit you." I laughed. "I hate you." "Come on let's go somewhere." I was hesitant. The only place I go is to therapy and yesterday when I went to his office. I was my first time going anywhere. "Where to." It's a surprised." We walked out to his car and I just stood there. "Come on it's not like I'm some stranger telling you I have candy in my car. Get in." Shawn said point to his car. "Shawn I'm not so sure about this." He walked over to me and grabbed my hands. "La'Rayna I will not let anything happen to you I promise." I held up my pinky and he laughed. This is something that we've been doing since we were kids. He twined his with mines. "I promise."

The drive to where ever we were going was pretty quiet. Shawn wasn't saying much I guess he didn't want to spoil where we were going because he knew I would ask questions. We couldn't listen to the radio because of what happened back at camp. I started to hear singing and laughing. "Never go over the hill...soon your soul will end...the cabin is at a dead end...cabin six that is...searching through the wasteland that is...they never found his body...now he's hunting everybody... you'll be next...he's coming for you with an ax...living at Camp Lakeview...gotta sleep with one eye open...or he's gonna get you." I looked over at Shawn who seemed to not hear anything. "Shawn." "Yeah." "Did you hear that?" "Hear what." He glanced over at me for a second. "Never mind."

**10**

**CHAPTER 10**

After being yelled at by Cutlip we were back in the nurse cabin getting my ankle checked out. Counselor Sarah came in to speak with us. "What were you kids doing out there in the woods alone?" None of us said anything. "I know Cutlip yelled at you and he can be a little mean but I'm only hear to help you guys." "We were looking for big foot!" Kirk shouted. Leave it to Kirk to come up with the most dumbest answer. "If you can't be honest with me we may have to call your parents." "We were just going on a hike we didn't think it would be such a big deal; I mean it was free time right? There was nothing planned and we were going has a group so we didn't see any harm in it. You know if we were looking out for each other." Yes, there you go Shawn saving the day. "Now how did you get hurt. And I want La'Rayna to answer not anyone else." I could tell she was sensing that we were lying but we weren't we did go on a hike we just did more than hike. "Well we were going hiking like Shawn said and I tripped over a rock and fell." "Are you okay?" "Yes, I'm fine see," I said standing up. It hurt a little bit but it wasn't too bad. The nurse came back into the room and gave me some ice to put on my foot. "Sit sit," she said fussing at me. "Now I want you to keep ice on your foot to help the swelling go down and keep your leg elevated." "Yes ma'am."

We headed back to our cabins. Danielle and Shawn helped me get back to cabin five. I couldn't help but think about Melissa like where did she sneak off to and letting us take the blame for everything. Boy I really can't stand that girl. Once we reached cabin five the door swung wide open. "Oh my goodness La'Rayna what happened to you," said Susie H. "Nothing I just fell and sprang my ankle." "Can you move please she's not light you know." I glared at Danielle. "How rude." She laughed. "But your not I know your shorter than me but you are 12 not 2 your kind of heavy for me." "I got her." Shawn said taking all my weight and helping me inside to my bed. "Well well guess who's back." I looked up to see that Melissa was sitting on her bed with that stupid grin on her face. "What ever do you mean?" "Don't give me that you know what I'm talking about. what happened to you out there?" "Out where I've been here all day haven't I Susie." "I wouldn't know I went fishing but when I came back you guys were gone and Melissa was sitting right here." "See I've been here all day." "No you haven't you were out there with us on that stupid hike that you dutch us on and letting us take the fall." Danielle spat I could tell she was growing tried of her lies. I don't know what that girl is hiding but I'm going to find out.

"Never go over the hill...soon your soul will end...the cabin is at a dead end...cabin six that is...searching through the wasteland that is...they never found his body...now he's hunting everybody...you'll be next...he's coming for you with an ax...living at Camp Lakeview...gotta sleep with one eye open...or he's gonna get you." Kirk, Kyle, and Josh sang as they came into my cabin with Danielle. Shawn stayed by my side for the rest of the day since I couldn't get up and walk yet. "Ugh would you guys stop singing that stupid song." "It's not stupid your stupid." "Don't start you two," Shawn chimed in. "What song?" I asked out of curiosity. "A song that a few people made up a while back because of uh you know what happened with the killer and all." Kyle said. First time I heard him speak without being Kirks echo. "So why are you guys singing the song?" Shawn asked. "Who knows once the song gets stuck in your head you sing it for no reason besides everyone is." "If everyone jump off a bridge would you?" I mumbled. Hoping his answer would be yes. I know that's harsh but they get on my nerves. Shawn heard me because he looked over at me. I mouthed what and he just shook his head while lightly chuckling. "We can teach you guys the song if you want." "Now why would we want to learn the song." "It's kind of tradition."

"Shawn get your friends" Danielle said. I could see she was getting tried of hanging with them. Since I couldn't walk and Shawn was keeping me company those are the only people she had left to hang around. Susie H keeps going off to who knows where and who wants to hang out with Melissa. So She did a coin toss and ended up with Kirk and his minions. "Why are you guys so scary?" Kirk asked. "Scary your the one to talk Kirk. You know what I'm not about to be bothered with you." "But its just a song." "A song about us maybe dying out here." I suggested. He shrugged. "So what its just to scary new campers. I admit thats all this stuff is okay. Its just to scare you guys. Its a tradition it happens ever year. It happened the year I started. Do you think they will keep a camp open if people went missing every year?" Well when he put it like that I guess not. Everything kind of does make sense now. But still what if...

"Do you think they will keep a camp open if people went missing every year?" I mumbled. "Huh?" Shawn asked. "Nothing just thinking about something." Looking out the window. "La'Rayna I heard what you said. I even heard what you said back at the house but I let it slide but this time I'm not. Whats going on with you?" He said while still driving to whatever the destination was. "I don't know why isn't that the reason for me going to see a shrink?" "Well if you can get smart then maybe everything that you are doing is just a game." "A game." I questioned him. "Yeah a game like you are still trying to get attention from happened. Since your dad left." I stopped him. I can't believe the things he was saying to me. "What is wrong with. Huh why would I want to get attention from this Shawn. Tell me uh who wants that kind of attention?" I yelled at him. He was starting to get on my nerves. He pulled over. "I don't know you tell me" He yelled at me. I slapped him so hard across his face the corner of his mouth started to bleed. I have never put my hands on him before. The shock and hurt in his eyes made me feel even worse. I held my hand over my mouth that was now ajar from the shock of me putting my hands on him. "I'm so sorry Shawn." I reached for his hand but he pulled away from me. I grabbed a napkin from the glove department and reach to clean the blood that was trickling down from the side of his mouth. When I reach over he flinched. "I'm not going to hurt you." "Oh really could've fooled me." He said side eyeing me. "Shawn I am really sorry I don't know what came over me." "Yeah me either." I frowned. "Whats thats supposed to mean." "You're not the same person I met La'Rayna." He started up the car again and pulled off. "Well Camp Lakeview changed me." He shook his head. "I'm starting to get tried of it. You're so selfish." "How am I being selfish." "Your not the only one that was out there you know. I lost people that I loved as well. I was almost killed too you know. You don't think what happened out there doesn't mess with me in the head. But..." He started. "But what?" "What happened to you?"

The rest of the car ride was silent. I can't believe that I hit Shawn. But the look in his eyes and what he said to me hurt me more than when I hit him. I never thought how things may have affected Shawn. He was so busy worrying and trying to protect me that he pushed everything that he was going through just to make sure that I was ok. Not once did I ask him if he was ok.

I only thought about myself. I was selfish and didn't even know it. I looked up at him. "I'm really sorry Shawn. For everything." He didn't say anything he just kept on driving.  I couldn't stand for him to be mad at me. So, grabbed his hand with mines. He started to rub his thumb across the back of my hand. He pulled it closer to his face and kissed it. "I could never be mad at you." It was like he was reading my mind like always.

I looked out the window and couldn't believe that we were here. Coming back to this place brought back painful memories. I have no idea what Shawn was thinking. "Remember this place." "How could I forget." I turned and looked at him and he was smiling. He got out the car and went around to my side and opened the door. "Come on get out." He reached in to grab my hand and helped me out." I hesitated took his hand and stepped out. "Shawn what are we doing here?" "Why whats wrong? I thought you would like being here. I mean look at it. Isn't it beautiful out here. Hasn't changed a bit." He said taking in all of our surroundings. He's right it hasn't changed a bit. We used to come here all the time when we were kids. "I want to go home now." "Look La'Rayna you are going to have to move past this and stop living in the past. I know it hurts but you are hurting yourself by not moving on. Danielle wouldn't want this. She didn't sacrifice her life for you to be stuck." "I know but this place just reminds me of all the times we had out here together." "Well try and remember all the good times we had."

He went to the back of his car and opened the truck pulling out a picnic basket. "Come on." I grabbed his hand and we went over to the willow tree. Our usually spot for just the three of us; the two of us now. He pulled out a blanket and sat it down. He then took out a picture of Danielle and say it in the far corner in the shade. I smiled because Danielle loved the shade so I knew thats why he put it there. "Still our spot." I lightly whispered. He sat down on the blanket and I laid my head in his lap while he ran hi finger through my hair. Times like these make me miss Danielle even more. "You know I miss her too."

**11**

—— ◆ ——

## CHAPTER 11

"Shawn stop!" I yelled at him. "Ugh you play too much." "Aw come its just water." "I'm black does it look I care. Getting my hair wet." "You didn't use to mind." I didn't use to mind a lot of things. "Well now my hair is straight, not its old curly afro." "Man black girls and they're hair." I splashed water on him. "Shut up." "Oh so you can get me wet but I can't get you wet." "Uh duh." He gave me this look. I know this look. I slowly backed up. "Shawn don't, I was only kidding." I pleaded waving my hands in front of me. Next thing I know we were in a splash war. I didn't care about getting my hair wet anymore I was having too much fun. I haven't had fun like this in a long time. I haven't smiled or laughed like this in a long time either and it felt good.

After we were done playing in the lake we went fishing by the dock. "This is nice. Thanks for this Shawn. I really needed this." "Anything for you." "I'm thankful for you." He smiled down at me. "I'm the lucky one" He said.

"Shawn come on I'm hungry." We have eaten the food that was in the picnic basket over and hour ago and I was starving.

"Well I'm trying to catch something to eat." "We've been out here all day and you haven't caught a thing. Come on let's go. We can get something back home." I whined. He was being a pain trying to get catch us some food." "Oh stop whining." "Tell you what if we leave now I promise we can go camping for real for real like we used to do when we were kids." He started to chew on his bottom lip like he does when he's debating on something. "I don't know I doubt you would go out again." He mumbled the last part. "Shawn I know that I haven't been the same but I will try. I will try for you." "La'Rayna I'm going to need you to try for yourself. Only if you promise me you will get better." "I promise." "Okay come on."  "Yes, finally we're leaving." "Not quite first hike then leave." "Aw that wasn't a part of the deal and I'm hungry." "Its a short hike, besides I have snacks in my bag." "You couldn't tell me that earlier?" "If I have would we still have snacks for this hike?" I looked down. "Exactly." He exclaimed.

   "Shawn," I said whining. "You have been playing all day now give me some." I wad trying to snatch the trail mix out of his hand. But he was too fast and I couldn't reach his grasp being that he towered over me. "Ugh you're so annoying." He laughed while handing me the bag of trail mix. "Here." I slowly reached for them expecting him to pull away again. He laughed. "Here take them." I started to eat some of the snack. "Shawn." "Yes." "Thanks for dragging me out here. I feel like my old self. It was fun." "Glad to know that I'm getting you back." He said as he grabbed my hand and kissing the back know of it.

We continued to walk down the trail hand in hand. I started getting these feelings that I haven't had in a long time. I felt like someone was watching us. I turn around but nothing was there. "Shawn how much further do we have left?" "Not much why?" "Because I'm getting tried of walking." I lied. I turned around again. "La'Rayna are you okay." "Yes, I'm fine." "Then why do you keep peeping over your shoulder?" "I'm just enjoying my surroundings. You know taking everything in. We haven't been here in years. I just miss being out doors." I lied. I could tell that he could tell that I was lying but he let it slide. He took one last glance at me and we continued to walk. I heard some rustling in the bush that made me paused pulling back on Shawns arm a little. Once I stopped so did Shawn. "La'Rayna are you okay?" "Did you hear that." "Hear what?" "Something moving in the bushes." "I didn't hear a thing but we uh can leave now if you think it's uh something else you know." He hesitated. "No, maybe I'm just being parionoid." "Look La'Rayna I was there too okay. If you feel like something is off we can go." Shawn was right. He experienced just as much as me if not more. He knew better to say oh it was just a rabbit in the bush or oh well are in the woods what do you expect to hear. He and I both know what could be in the woods. There was no time to play blah white kid in a scary movie. You either act or die. But I'm trying to get better. Better for me and better for Shawn. Besides nothing could possibly be going on in these woods we been coming here for years.

"Shawn it's nothing. We been having a nice time out here. I don't want to ruin it." "La'Rayna." "Shawn it's okay I'm fine I'm just being parionoid. I'm not use to this anymore," I said cutting him off. "Okay fine but let me know and we can leave." He started to walk off again. I glanced to my left real quick and something shinning in the sun light caught my eye. Curiosity killed the cat I thought to myself. Um but I'm not a cat. I headed towards the shiny object. I pushed past the bushes that led me off the dirt pathway and into a grasses blazed surround by more tress and bushes. I bent down to pick up the object until I felt I pair of hands on me. I jump back and screamed hitting away at whatever it was that grabbed me. "Its me La'Rayna it's me." The familiar voice shouted. I looked up and it was Shawn. "Oh my gosh don't ever do that again you scared the crap out of me." I said with one hand on my chest breathing heavy. "I scared you man you scared me. I was walking and talking to you. When you didn't answer I didn't know what happened to you." "I'm sorry I just seen this thing flashing in my face." I looked around for it. Once I seen the object is picked it up and rubbed some of the dirt off it. It was a women's necklace. I frowned. "Um What would this be doing out here. It looked new." I said to Shawn but he didn't respond. "Shawn." I questioned. I looked up at him. He had a shocked look on his face staring into the distance. I tried to follow his gaze.

Doing so I wish I never did. There laid a women face down covered in blood. The sight looked all to familiar sadly. "I'm sorry Danielle." I whispered.

We run and jump and swim and play we row and go on trips but the thing that last forever is the bloody shed. Camp Lakeview is known for a killer that seeks after the campers for whatever reason. Nobody knows what or who it is. I always like horror movies but never thought I would live in one.

I'm so scared I don't know what to do. I can't stop crying. I can't believe my best friend is gone. My best friend is dead and I don't know what happened to my other best friend. He told me to stay and wait for him. He said he would be back but he never came. I was sitting in the bush until I heard a noise. I tried to stay quiet but I had to act or I probably be dead by now. Out here you either act or die I was almost caught. I said I wouldn't peek out but then I heard someone calling for help. I knew who it was so I climbed put to help them. They started to stagger towards me. I reached my arm out to grab there hand. She just reached the tip of my fingers. I got a glimpse of her now dark blue eyes. They used to be bright  as the sky. She locked eyes with mines then froze and fell face down in the ground. I jumped back and screamed when I seen the knife in her back. "Oh no Su." I tried to get out. No words left my mouth. I knew I had to get out of there. Whatever or whoever must of heard my screams. I dash all the while hiding behind tree after tree to take a breather and so I wouldn't be seen. I made it to

McKinley Dinning Hall. The place where we sat and ate, telling stories from our day earlier at camp, and just simply goofing off. I looked across the empty room just thinking  how we will never get a chance to do it again. It's not like the room was the same anyways there was blood everywhere. I heard a loud crash outside and ran straight to the back to hide. Once I reach the back there she was laying faced down covered in blood. I fell to my knees in front of her and picked up her necklace.

**12**

CHAPTER 12

The red and blue lights can be seen flashing between the tree branches. They shined even brighter now that it was getting dark outside. I sat on the hood of the car with a blanket wrapped around me while I stare off in the distance. I can't believe the horror surprise that laid out in front of me. I never thought I would be in a situation like this again yet here I am. Shawn was over speaking to the police. I could only image what this lady went threw. And its too familiar imagery I didn't want playing in my head. I looked over to where her body laid. They were still taking pictures of her. I felt disgusted. It was like they were disrespecting her but it had to be done.

I felt a presence someone walk over to me and stand behind me. "Such a lonely heart lyin in wait." I whispered. "Hello, La'Rayna I'm detective Dan." I didn't look his way. He cleared his throat and continued. "May I ask you a few questions? We already spoken to your friend Shawn. He told us that you discovered the body. Is that correct?" I shook my head indicating yes. "Can you tell us exactly what you saw when you first seen the body?" I shrugged my shoulders not certain on what to say.

I mean I couldn't really say anything. Seeing her body laying on the ground brought back unwanted memories that I was trying to erase. Plus I don't like speaking to people I don't know.

"Um Sir." I heard Shawn say. "She doesn't speak." "Well she's going to have to we have questions that need to be answered." "I don't think you understand." "No I don't think you understand she needs to answer these questions or else we can take her down to the station and she can sit in a cell until she decides to talk." Shawn was about to speak again until I cut him off. "I found her laying on the ground face down. No I don't know her. That should answer your questions." I hopped down off the hood of car and walked off. I could still hear Shawn finish speaking with the officer. Soon enough he caught up with me. "La'Rayna are you okay?." "Yes, I'm fine I'm ready to go." "That guy was a jerk. I had to tell him a few things." "Its okay I don't want to talk about him anymore. I just want to go home I'm tried."

The car ride back home was silent. Not a peaceful silence more of an errie silence. I'm sick of feeling like this. Today was a nice day. I haven't had fun like that in forever. I thought things could maybe just somehow go back to normal. But death just seems to follow me everywhere I go now. "What are you thinking about?" Shawn asked snapping me out of my thoughts. "About today." "I'm sorry." "Shawn it's not your fault." "I know. It's just I know we can never seem to get a break. And someone has to apologize. Even if you get it from the one who didn't cause the pain." I looked at him while his eyes stayed on the road; causing me to only see the side of his face. I admire this man so much. To go through what we went through at such a young age and still be so positive about everything. "Have I ever told you that I love you?" He chuckled. "I know, I know." "Umph cocky." I said under my breath.

We finally made it home. I was ready to lay down and relax. I wanted to forget about the things that occur today. I wanted to go back to the time that we were happy. Sometimes the best way to move past your past is to live in your present and live towards your future. I know what I have to do in order for me to move on.

I got out of bed and walked down the hall to Shawns room. I knocked on the door. He told me to come in. I opened the door a little bit to peak my head in. "Sorry did I wake you?" "If you don't get in here and quit acting like that." He told me. I stepped in and slowly closed the door a day stood by it. "Come over here." He waved me over. I walked over and sat on the edge of the bed. "Why you acting like this? Come here." He grabbed me by my waist to pull me closer to him. I giggled and removed his hand. "Because I want to talk about something important." He sat up and looked at me. "What's up is something wrong?" I took a deep breath. "No, it's nothing. I just want to help you with everything." I looked down "Help with what?" "The camp. I want help with the camp." "Are you serious?" I looked up at him and shook my head indicating yes. He looked over my face to see if I was being real with him. "Am I dreaming?" "Shawn I'm being serious." I whined. "I am too. A few weeks ago you weren't talking to me when you found out that the camp was reopening now you want to help." "Yes, this is my trying." I whispered looking back down. He grabbed my chin and lifted my head back up causing me to look into his eyes. "I like your trying." "Really." "Yeah I think its a great way to start your healing. Besides only God knows that I need some help. Stuff is stressful. Especially getting all the blueprints to come to life. I can't what until you see the camp." "Uh no." "No what?" "I'm not going back out there." "You just said." Cutting him off. "I know what I said. I can help from afar. First things first looking at the blueprints." "Well sooner or later you have to go see the camp." I leaned back into his bed getting comfortable. He snuggled up next to me and kissed my temple. "Little itty-bitty steps," I said. "Okay little itty-bitty steps it is then. Little itty-bitty steps," He said.

I'm glad with my choice. I know it's what Danielle would want for me. "Keeping her memory alive," Shawn said. "I wish you wouldn't do that." "Do what?" "Read my mind." "I can't help it if we are thinking the samething. "Whatever and go to sleep." "Go to sleep? I was until you barged your fat butt in here," He said smacking it. "Ow keep your hands to yourself Mr. And I'm not fat." "Naw but your butt is." He started rubbing it. "Ugh stop before I go back to my room." "I can't help it. It's so soft." "Goodbye." He laughed. "Okay I'll stop." He pulled me back down. "You can be so annoying." "I thought we were moving past that don't make me put you out." "Whatever," I said yawning. "Shawn." "Um." "Can we switch beds your bed is so comfy." "Go to sleep La'Rayna."

# 13

## CHAPTER 13

Never go over the hill...soon your soul will end...the cabin is at a dead end...cabin six that is...searching through the wasteland that is...they never found his body...now he's hunting everybody...you'll be next...he's coming for you with an ax...living at Camp Lakeview...gotta sleep with one eye open...or he's gonna get you."

"So what do you plan on doing with cabin six?" "What do you mean?" "What do you guys plan on doing with that cabin. You know what that place was." "Oh that, well I wanted to knock it down but." he trailed off looking elsewhere. I stood in front of him and grabbed his face forcing him to look at me. "But what?" "But my father wants to leave it as it is." "What." I yelled at him. "Well not excatly how it is. He wants to polish it up a bit and turn it into the merchinse store." "What is wrong with that man. How could he? Reopening the camp was one thing now this." "I know, I tried to talk him out of this but he shut me down. He said if I wanted to do whatever I wanted for the camp that would be his only say so." "Still doesn't make it right."

I woke up to the bright sun shining in my face. We have officaily been at camp for a full two weeks now. Nothing too strange has happened, so I guess it's safe to say that what Kirk told us was a lie. My ankle is still a little banged up but at least the swollen has gone down. I still can't walk on it for too long. Shawn has made me this really cool crutch out of a stick. Today, we were going swimming which I'm glad because I love to swim, also, it will help with my sore ankle.

"Hey, La'Rayna are you ready to go?" Danielle asked. "Yes, I'm just have to put my shoes on then we can go." "Is your ankle alright?" "Yeah it should be fine for swimming." We headed out the door and down to the lake. "I'm so glad that you are okay. I was getting real sick and tired of flipping a coin to see who I had to hang out with. Kirk and his crew are so annoying. Susie H is a little strange. And you know how I feel about Melissa." Suise H can't be that bad." "Oh shes the worst. Something isn't right about her. I don't really trust her. She's always going off by herself and not telling anybody where. Who knows what she could be doing." "Now who's paranoid." "Hey, maybe you were right about this place." I stopped in my tracks. Nothing strange has been going on since we went on that stupid hike. "Danielle what do you mean?" "I mean the person that nobody believes is always right. Then everyone else ends up dead right." "Danielle this isn't a horror movie." "Could be. I'm just sick of this place already. With these creepy campers, creepy staff, and that stupid creepy cabin six." "You got that right. I guess we are just ready to go home." "Ohh look at you." "What?" "Growing into your big girl panties I like this new La'Rayna." "Oh whatever." I laughed at her.

We finally made it to the lake. The lake was so beautiful. I think it's the best part about the camp. The only downside about the lake is that cabin six sits right on the other side. If you don't pay attention to that the lake is really nice.

"Took you guys long enough." Shawn yelled at us. He was starting to get out of the water. "Hey La'Rayna was trying to get cute." "Shut up no I wasn't." I pushed her. "Yeah you were." "For who." "Shawn." My eyes grew big. "Shut up I do not like Shawn." I don't know what would make her think that. "It's okay if you do." "Danielle that's not funny." "What's not funny?" Shawn asked once he reached us. "Nothing." I pushed Danielle again as she poked me in my side. "Are you guys getting in or what? The water's nice." "Yeah." We both said.

Get got in the water inch by inch. You know how you have to ease your way into water because it's so cold because your not use to it. "Man, come in guys." "It's cold." "It's not cold." "That's because you've been in there for a while." Shawn swammed over by me putting his hand out. "Come on, grab my hand." I gave him a look. "You trust me right?" I reached out and grabbed his hand. He pulled me right in getting me all wet. "Ugh its so cold. I hate you." "But you love me." He smiled. "Whatever." I splashed him with water. and so the war began. "Okay I give up." I swam back over to the dock. I look over and Danielle was just smiling. "What?" "I told you." "I do not like Shawn." "Sure you don't." "Why are you saying this all of a sudden?" "It's not really all of a sudden. You guys would be cute together." "We are just friends." "Whatever you say La'Rayna whatever you say."

It was bright and warms. The fire crackling on the wood. The air was warm but it was still nice. We sat out by the campfire singing songs, playing games, and roasting marsh mellows. It was nice. I felt like we were finally enjoying camp. Kirk and them were still annoying but at least the stupid killer stoires stopped. However, after what Danielle told me this morning, those feelings about camp were starting to come back. Not only that, but I did find an id bracelat in cabin six. What if that belonged to Melissa missing brother. I want to tell Shawn and Danielle about it but I don't want to ruin anything. Not when we just started having fun.

"Are you okay?" "Yeah I was just thinking." "About what?" "About all the fun that we have been having. I'm really starting to enjoy camp." "See I told you didn't I?" Shawn said as he nedge my arm with his elbow. I smiled at him. "Yeah you did." I look over at Danielle and she mouths "I told you." I shook my head at her. "Shawn you need to get your friend." "Who?" "Danielle, she has this crazy idea that we would look cute together." I said putting air quotes around cute together." "Ah maybe." He put his arm around me. "What does that mean?" "It means what you want it to mean." "You two make me sick."

"But you love us." That I do. I lean into him. "Shawn I have something to tell you." "What is it?" "Well, uh it's about cabin six."

## 14

## CHAPTER 14

"**S**hawn I have something to tell you." "What is it?" "Well, uh it's about cabin six."

"What do you mean you have to tell me something about cabin six? I thought we were over this?" "I am. It's just that." "Just what, what could possibly be going on? I thought we agreed to enjoy camp and not worry about those stupid stories." "We did but I found something." "What could you have possibly found? Uh La'Rayna what?" "I found this I.D bracelet. It was hidden inside one of those drawers that time we went inside." "Why is this important?" "I don't know. I just feel like there is something more to that cabin then what has been lead on. Why keep the cabin up and abandon? Why not tear it down or fix it up? It not just a stupid story to scare new campers." "La'Rayna I don't want to hear about it anymore." "Why not?" "Because it's stupid." "No, you are just afraid. You are afraid that I might be right." "You know what fine. To prove to you how ridiculous this is. How about we go back to cabin six? We can go back tonight. After everyone has gone to sleep we will sneak back into cabin six and show you that nothing is going on here. Then maybe you finally be able to leave your delusions behind." "So now I'm delusional." "La'Rayna." "Save it," I yelled at him. "We will go and I will prove you wrong." I stormed off.

I can't believe he would call me delusional. I know that what I'm saying may sound a little out there but to call me delusional was another story. It really hurt my feelings that my best friend would call me delusional. We are supposed to be having fun at camp I get that but I will never get over this feeling that I have. There is something going on at this camp and I'm going to find out what it is that everyone seems to be hiding.

We decided to meet up at night to sneak into cabin six. There was no way we could meet during the day if we didn't want to get caught. After, the campfire everyone will be getting ready for bed. Our camp counselor won't check the cabin until 10. So we should have plenty of time to sneak in and out. "Come on La'Rayna. If we plan on making it back in time then we have to leave now," Danielle whispered to me. "I'm coming." I reached down in my bag and grabbed the i.d bracelet. Once I slipped it into my pocket and headed out the door. It was easy for her to leave because Melissa was in the shower and Susie H was in the bathroom as well. We already acted as if we were so tired from earlier in the day. So, we took our showers early and faked went to bed.

"I cannot believe that we are actually doing this. Especially you La'Rayna being that you are a scary cat." "I'm not a scary cat I just don't like being scared." "What do you think we are going to find?" "I don't know. I already told Shawn about this but I did find something." Danielle stopped and her eyes widened. "What do you mean you found something. Well, what is it?" "Well, you know the first time we went into cabin six right?" "Yeah." "I found this i.d bracelet in the dresser." I pulled the i.d bracelet out of my pocket and handed it to her. "I also thought that I have seen something in the closet but you wanted to leave so bad I didn't have time to check it out." "Girl you were there it smelled so bad in there."

We continued walking. We were meeting up with Shawn outside of cabin six. Once we reached the other side of the lake where cabin six lay we stopped. "Where is he?" "I don't know he said he would meet us right here." "Wait what is this?" "What?" "This spot on the i.d bracelet? There is a name on here but this spot is covering it up." "I don't know I tried to see what it was as well." "So, what do you think this will tell us?" "I'm not too sure. Whoever names is on that bracelet maybe could tell us who stayed in that cabin. It's just a feeling I have." "I get it. I've noticed too. Its like someone is out here watching us."

"Boo!" "Ahhh!" Dani screamed. I just stood there because I knew it was Kirk with his dumb prank. I crossed my arms and put all of my weight on one foot. Shawn and Kirk started laughing. "Ugh, you guys get on my nerves," Danielle yelled at them. "What is he doing here anyways." "He wanted to tag along." "For what?" "I want to go ghost hunting too. Why do you guys get to have all the fun?" "We are not going ghost hunting you idioit." Kirk and Danielle could go on and on. "Are we here to look for clues are are we here to play games?" "Ohh look who grew some balls." "Shut up Kirk." "Oh come on Ray Ray." I cut him off. "Stop calling me that." "Okay guys we didn't come here for that. Lets just go."

We all walked over to cabin six and up onto the porch. Before we went in Shawn stopped us. "Come on man what are we waiting for," Kirk complained. "Before we walk in I want to give you guys this. Here you go." "What is it?" "It's to clean that spot off the i.d bracelet." "Shawn I think its rust. It's not going to come off." "Yeah, and why did you bring a can of coke?" "That's why I brought this. Coke can clean almost anything." I opened up the can of pop. Shawn took the can and poured it on the napkin he has brung and wiped it on the bracelet. "I'll take that." "Kirk said taking the can of pop and drinking it. "Kirk," Danielle said with an annoyed tone. "What we don't need it anymore. Besides, I'm throisty." I shook my head and laughed at him. "Jake," Shawn said barely above a whisper. "What?" I semi-yelled while snatching the i.d bracelet out of his hand. I looked at the bracelet and in fact, it did say, Jake. Danielle looked between Shawn and I with an confused exrpession. "Whats going on who is Jake?" "I guess thats what we are going to find out," said Shawn.

# 15

## CHAPTER 15

"Jake," Shawn said barely above a whisper. "What?" I semi-yelled while snatching the i.d bracelet out of his hand. I looked at the bracelet and in fact, it did say, Jake. Danielle looked at Shawn and me with a confused expression. "Whats going on who is Jake?" "I guess that's what we are going to find out," said Shawn.

It's crazy to hear and read that name. Jake, Jake was just a dream that I had. It couldn't possibly be more than that. I thought at one point there was someone named Jake at the camp. That's why I had the dream and asked about him before. But this is just too weird. "Oh, thats Melissa brothers name." We all turned to look over at Kirk in shock. "What did you say," said Shawn. "You guys were wondering who Jake was. Its Melissa's brother. I don't see the big deal." Kirk said with a shrug of his shoulders. "What do you mean its not a big deal? Melissa brother is the guy that everyone said went missing. La'Rayna found this bracelet in cabin six. and for some strange reason that Shawn and La'rayna already heard of this name," Danielle said frustrated. "What, I was drinking my coke." "You are a real piece of work you know that." Before they could go back and forth Shawn intervene. "Guys enough we are not about to get any answer by arguing." "Shawn is right. Lets just do what we came to do," I added.

We headed towards cabin six. I wasn't too sure about this but we needed to find out what was going on at the camp. "Wait why are we going in there?" Kirk asked. "What are you scared?" "What no I've been in there plenty of times." "Well, this shouldn't be a problem now should it. Lets go." "Wait if you want information I can give it to you." "What kind of information could you possibly give us?" "Okay, so Jake is Melissa's brother." "Right, you told us this already," Danielle said cutting him off. "Let me finish. Jake is Melissa's brother that went missing. He didn't just go missing like the camp claims. He most definitely was killed by the camp killer. And the camp paid off Melissa's family. Why do you think the treat her so well here?"

So Kirk told us nothing. That was something we already suspected. Also, that information wasn't enough to tell us what is really going on at this camp. If I wanted answers I was going to have to go back into cabin six. I headed up the stairs. "La'Rayna where are you going?" "I want more answer than what Mr. Stating the obvious gave us." "Yeah and we are wasting time guys. We have to get back to out cabins before the next check," said Shawn.

Shawn opened the door and we walked right on in. "I'm not going in there." "Come on." Danielle reached out and pulled Kirk by his collar inside the cabin. "Ugh it smells ten times worse than the last time." "How is that even possible?" "What exactly are we looking for?" "Last time we were in here I seen a stack of papers." We all turned to look at Danielle. "Why didn;t you tell us this before?" She shrugged her shoulders. "I didn't think nothing of it before. Besides, I wasn't able to see what the papers were because we left out."

The rest of them walked over to the stack of papers that Danielle was talking about. I wanted to see what was in  the closet.  I put my hand on the rusty doorknob and took a deep breath. I just hoped nothing pops out of here. As I was about to open the door I hears Danielle yell. "Are you kidding me?" "What?" "All of these papers are our letters home." "That can't be right." "Take a look for yourself." I was about to walk over to where they were until I heard something fall in the closet; whivh made me jump. "What was that?" Kirk said all scared. "I don't know it sounded like it came from the closet. "Thats it I'm getting out of here." "Quit being such a baby." "I'm not being a baby I'm being smart. If you knew what was good for you then you will leave too." "Hey what is that supposed to mean?"? Shawn asked. He didn't take threats too lightly escapilly threats to us. "It means what it means." With that Kirk left out of the cabin.

"If we are leaving I'm going to take these letters. We can check them all out tomoorow." "Wait, let me at least check to see what fell in the closet."  I turned back around and opneed the closet door. I shine my flashlight inside. On the floor there was a book. The back of the closet there was a hole. Too small for anyone of us to go through. I picked the book off the floor and felt something wet and sticky on the bottom. I shined my flashlight at the back of the book. "Ew!" I yelled. Shawn and Danielle came running over. "What is it?" "Is that blood?"

**16**

— • —

## CHAPTER 16

The camp has been coming along just great. It's expected to open in a few weeks. Kids from all over the country have already signed up to go. Shawn had hired the staff to run the camp. Things are going just great. I still haven't been yet and I don't plan on it. I have been helping Shawn with the plans right here at home. I tried to get them to change the name from Camp Lakeview to Camp Creekwood. I don't know just something different to have a fresh start but Shawns dad was very adamant to keep the name the same. He said something about persevering history and changing people's perspectives from what happened years ago. Making people see that Camp Lakeview wasn't original a horror camp but what the camp stood for blah blah.

I went into Shawn's room to see him packing. "Where are you going?" "I have to go out to the camp and make sure everything is going great. With the grand opening is in a few days so I need to get out there as soon as possible." "And when were you going to tell me this?" "I just found out myself. My dad was going to go out there but he has to go to another property so that leaves me." "How long are you going to be gone?" "Until the opening." I sat down on his bed. He stopped packing and came over and sat next to me. "You should come with me." I looked at him like he was crazy. There was no way that I could go back to that camp. "I don't think that I can step foot back in the camp." "I think it would be good for you. Good for the both of us. I feel like we can finally move on. I haven't been yet but we changed a lot of things about the camp. They layout isn't the same. It would be like we are looking at a different camp. I'll be there so you won't be alone." "I don't." "Danielle would want you to go." "Stop using the Danielle card," I said hitting him with a pillow. I knew he was right I couldn't keep moping around. It will not bring her back. I can't keep letting life pass me by because of what happened in the past. Danielle didn't save my life for me to sitting around and be depressed. "I guess. Only on one condition. We have to have something to celebrate all the people who have died."

Driving to Camp Lakeview was pretty fun. I let Shawn play music in the car. We sung along to songs on the radio. Mostly I just listened to Shawn singing. I loved to hear his voice. If he didn't work for his dad I would suggest  that he try to get into the entertainment business. He can really sing. We talked about a lot of things. I haven't been talking a lot since what happened years ago. It just felt great to get back to my old self once again.

We pulled up the camp. I was kind of nervous. We haven't been here in 15 years. The camp will open in a few days. The exact day 15 years ago that we went to camp. Shawn got out the car. I stayed in to take a few deep breaths. You can do it. You can get out of the car. My car door opened and I knew it had to be Shawn. "Are you getting out?" "Yes." He reached in for my hand to help me out of the car. It was so surreal. Standing in front of the entrance to the camp. Looking up at the wood sign with the words Camp Lakeview above our heads. I couldn't believe that I was back here. "Well, we have arrived. Lets go," Shawn said grabbing my hair.

**17**

CHAPTER 17

Shawn grabbed my hand and led me into the camp. I just couldn't believe that I was coming back to my worst nightmare. I had to get over it some kind of way. I was glad that I came. As we were walking to where ever we were walking to I looked around. Shawn was right the layout was different. I could still tell where things used to be but for the most part, the camp looked different. "Shawn where are you taking me?" "To the lake."

The lake was just a beautiful as it was the last time that I was here. The only downside as usually was cabin six. Cabin six stood on the other side of the lake like always looking exactly the same 15 years ago. "Shawn I thought you said that they were fixing cabin six up." I turned to look at him but he seemed so caught up in the lake. "Uh," Shawn said. "Cabin six it looks exactly the same." "It's supposed to look the same. They were supposed to just fix it up a bit." "It doesn't look like they fixed anything." Looking over at the lake Shawn noticed what I noticed. The cabin looked like not one person even laid hands on it to fix anything. I can tell that he was angry by the look on his face. He grabbed my hand and we begin walking over there. Now, that is one thing that I do not want to do. Be by cabin six.

Standing in front of the place that caused so many horrible memories. The fact that the place still looked the same as it did 15 years ago today did help. Shawn held the blueprints in his hand while talking on the phone. "I know the cabin is still supposed to be here but it's not supposed to look the same. It's like you guys didn't touch it all." Shawn yelled through the phone. "I don't care what my father said we had an agreement." With that he hung up the phone. He started rubbing his hand across his forehead letting out a huge sign. I walked over to him and grabbed his hands to calm him down. "Look I'm sorry. My father told them not to touch anything. However, my father told me they were to fix it up but keep the old look of the cabin. I can't believe he did this." "It's not you fault. It's too late to do anything now the camp opens in a few days." I turned to face the cabin. "Now, You said your father wanted to turn this into a store. Let's see how it turned out." I headed towards the cabin until Shawn grabbed my hand. "Whoa are you sure you want to go in there?" "Yes, I'm up to it. It's a new beginning." With that he grabbed my hand and led me inside cabin six.

Despite the outside of the cabin the inside was completely different. While I was looking around a guy came in to speak with Shawn. Where the dresser once was sat a counter. There was more light coming in from the outside. Where the closet onces was was not a storage unit. There was camp paraphernalia everywhere. It looked really nice. It kind of made up for the outside. Behind the counter there were pictures all over the back wall. I walked over to get a better look. Glancing at all the picture brought a smile to my face. It was nice to see all the old pictures if us at camp. There were even older pictures from when the camp first started up until when it closed 15 years ago. My eyes landed on a picture that I've never seen before. It was Shawn, Danielle, and I wearing our camp shirts with our arms around each other. I rubbed my fingertips over it. "You like it?" I jumped not realizing that Shawn was right behind me. "Don't do that." "I'm sorry. I didn't mean to." "So, how are you liking it." "Well, besides the outside I like it. It's completely different. I love this wall." "I knew you would. I found these pictures after they cleared everything from the camp. We were going through storages to see what to use and all of these old pictures were there. I have pictures placed all around the camp. Come on let me show you around."

Shawn led me all over the camp. The layout of the camp was still the same but all of the designs were different. I helped out with that part. Shawn father decided to keep some of the names the same but he changed each cabin number to reflect some of the victims that died that day.

We were now sitting in Shawn's office as he went over a few more details before the camp opens in a few days. I can see how much this camp as been stressing him out. Here I was moping around and being mad at him just for opening the place back up. I never thought about what he went through. I had seen my best friend murder right in front of my eyes. I don't know what Shawn went through or what he saw after he told me to run and hide. He never talks about it. He has alway been there for me and helping me out.

"Do you need any help?" He looked up at me and smiled. "Naw, I'm okay. You've done enough. You being here is enough." "Stop." "What I'm telling the truth. So, how do you like the camp." "I like it. I'm glad you guys took my advice about the designs." "You really have a knack for architect. You sure you don't want to work for my dad?" "As if." There was a knock at the door and Shawan security walked in. "Oh, um I'm sorry but Mr. Weiss There is a Mr. McCray outside waiting for you." Shawn and I both looked at each other. There is no way. We haven't heard from him in years. What was Kirk doing here?

# 18



## CHAPTER 18

I didn't understand what Kirk was doing here. We haven't heard from him in 15 years. Last that I heard of him was put in a psych ward. It was said that he was yelling and screaming that he was right the whole time but nobody believed him. It had gotten to the point where he would just yell I knew it over and over. Sometimes he would switch up his sayings. He kind of reminded me of myself. If it wasn't for my mother I might have been locked up as well. The things we went through were pretty traumatic for kids to go through.

"Old friend. It's nice to see you." He said looking at Shawn. I guess he didn't notice me. Shawn held the same confused expression on his face. "Kirk?" Shawn questioned. "It's me in the flesh." "What are you doing here? Last, I heard you were um getting better. I know that was a few years ago. I just didn't expect this. I didn't expect you to be here." I looked at Shawn trying to read him. It's likely that he knew what was going on in the outside world more than me. I was still trapped in the past. "I heard about the camp reopening so I decided hey why not check it out. Besides my niece is supposed to be attending.

I had to check it out. You know what happened her 15 years right?" He asked like we weren't there. "Look Kirk." "I'm just messing with you Shawn." He glanced over in my direction. Then did a double take. "Oh, and who might this be?" "You really don't know?" I asked. "No, but I'm sure I wouldn't forget a face as beautiful as yours." Okay so that was corny and awkward I didn't know how to respond. "That's La'Rayna Kirk." His eyes grew wide and he started coughing like he was choking on his own spit. "Oh um my apologies. I didn't recognize you. I mean look at you. You look different good. Better than I remember." "Thanks," I say sarscatily. I was not taking that as a compliment. Kirk was just as rude as ever.

I left and let Shawn and Kirk catch up. I walked around the camp and somehow I ended up here; The sunflower house formerly known as cabin five of the girls side of the camp. Sunflowers were Danielle favorite flower so Shawn and I decided to name the cabin after her. Just that thought made me smile. I walked the steps to the cabin. I took a deep breath to prepare myself to go in. I haven't been here in 15 years and that wasn't a very fond memory.

The cabin was brighter than I remember. The cabin was decorated beautifully sunflowers everywhere. It wasn't tacky like though. Sometimes sunflowers can come off tacky and old lady like but this wasn't. Standing in the middle of the cabin brought back unwanted memories. I started to see flashes of Danielle and myself screaming and running. I fell and she helped me up. The room became bright and I heard some-one yell. "La'Rayna!" There was blood everywhere. "La'Rayna," someone said and there was a hand placed on my shoulder. I jumped at the touch and turned around. "Are you okay?" "Yeah you just scared me. I didn't know you were there." "So, do you like how the place turned out." "Yes, its really nice." "Better than I expected.." I could see the excitement in his eyes. Its the first project that his dad left him have almost complete control over. It was a chance to show his dad that one day he could take over the company. "You are so excited aren't you?" "Yeah, I just can't wait for the camp to open up and have everyone see it after all of these years." "Yeah I bet. So, what did Kirk what?" His facial expression changed to something that I could not decipher. "Nothing really. He hasn't changed not one bit.But I do need to ask you something." "What is it?" "What is this celebration that you have planned." "Oh, I thought we could talk about that in your new office." I said using air quotes. "The office was my fathers idea." "Okay, okay."

We were in Shawns office going over the plans for the cele-bration. I wanted to do something to celebrate all the people that died 15 years ago. We decided on a candle light service the night before Camp Lakeview is supposed to open. We were going over the details. I was trying to keep it simple because I know Shawn already has a lot on his plate but he convinced me otherwise. Throwing the Danielle card again he mentioned that we had to do something big because of her. Shawn has been on and off the phone since we been in here trying to get everything handle before the opening.

I was sitting on the window seal of his office looking over some paperwork. I look up and Shawn was finally getting off the phone. He was so frustrated. "Is everything okay?" "Yeah, I just have to go check something out." "I can go look if you want." "No, its okay I can handle it. I'll be back. If you need anything call me okay." "Okay, just go." I got up and sat in Shawns big brown office chair. It was so comfortable that it made me want to fall alseep right in it. But I can't and I have to get back to work. I set the paperwork down and seen a brown envelope with Shawns name written on it in black letters it said important read admittedly. I didn't want to be nosy nut I couldn't help myself. I pulled out the first thing and it had a picture of all of us at camp. Susie H, Shawn, Danielle, Kirk and his minions and I. I turned the picture over and it said the past in red letters. I don't understand. What about the past?

**19**

**CHAPTER 19**

I was sitting on the window seal of his office looking over some paperwork. I look up and Shawn was finally getting off the phone. He was so frustrated. "Is everything okay?" "Yeah, I just have to go check something out." "I can go look if you want." "No, its okay I can handle it. I'll be back. If you need anything call me okay." "Okay, just go." I got up and sat in Shawn's big brown office chair. It was so comfortable that it made me want to fall asleep right in it. But I can't and I have to get back to work. I set the paperwork down and seen a brown envelope with Shawn's name written on it in black letters it said important read admittedly. I didn't want to be nosy but I couldn't help myself. I pulled out the first thing and it had a picture of all of us at camp. Susie H, Shawn, Danielle, Kirk and his minions and I. I turned the picture over and it said the past in red letters. I don't understand. What about the past?

"If we are leaving I'm going to take these letters. We can check them all out tomorrow." "Wait, let me at least check to see what fell in the closet." I turned back around and opened the closet door. I shine my flashlight inside. On the floor there was a book. The back of the closet there was a hole. Too small for anyone of us to go through. I picked the book off the floor and felt something wet and sticky on the bottom. I shined my flashlight at the back of the book. "Ew!" I yelled. Shawn and Danielle came running over. "What is it?" "Is that blood?"

I screamed and dropped the box. Shawn took off his shirt and wiped my hands with it. "Calm down guys." He held my hands trying to get me to calm down. "Look we are going to go back to the cabin with these letters and this box. We are going to figure out whats going on." He picked the box back up with his shirt and started to wipe it off. "Come on lets get out of here."

We made it back in time before the check-ins. We had to be very quite though because Susie and Melissa were sleeping. "Danielle," I whispered. "What?" She whispered back. "I don't think that I can go to sleep. Not after all of that stuff we found. And the blood. I can't forget about the blood." "La'Rayna everything will be okay. Tomorrow after breakfast we will go through everything and get to the bottom of this. You have to relax and go to sleep." "But what are we really getting ourselves into? We don't even know whats going on." "La'Rayna this was your idea." "I know but I'm scared." "It will be okay. We will figure it out tomorrow." With that we both went to sleep.

The next day at breakfast was really quiet between all of us. McKinley hall was thriving and booming with campers all over. I could hardly eat. I was pushing my food around my plate to pass the time. Just thinking about what this camp could be hiding and what all of this could mean. Like that book what could that book possibly be about. Why was there blood on the book? "La'Rayna are you ready to go?" "Huh." "I asked if you are ready to go. Breakfast is over." "Oh yeah."

We head back over to Shawn and Kirks cabin since they are the ones that took the book. This morning around seven they came over to our cabin to take the bag of letters that Danielle brought with her. It was easier to get the items since everyone was still sleeping and we didn't want Melissa and Susie to find out about them. "Before we go through anything we must make promises to each other," Shawn spoke up. "Promise about what?" "We have to promise that whatever we find here we will not tell another soul at this camp and that there is no turning back after we find out the truth." "We promise." All of us said.

There was no telling what could happen after we uncover the truth. This camp is hiding things from us. We are going to get to the bottom of it no matter what. I just knew something wasn't right about this camp. With the way the treat Melissa, not being able to call home all these crazy stories going around about a killer, missing campers, and cabin six. Now we find out that our letter may not have made it home and this book with blood on it. I have to know whats really going on with Camp Lakeview.

**20**

CHAPTER 20

S hawn, Kirk, and Danielle were going through all the letter. Once we realized that the camp wasn't sending home all of our letters. This whole situation was just strange. The only communication that we thought we were having with the outside world was proven to be false. So, they decided to go back to cabin six to see if they could find anything else. Who knows what they are hiding in that cabin. I didn't want to step foot inside cabin six let alone be by it. They agreed to let me stay behind. I'm still in Shawn and Kirks cabin reading the book that I found in the closet. The book was actually Jake journal.

"Did you guys hear what happened? "What." "Cash from cabin two went missing last night. They claim that he was sent home early because of bad behavior. But the funny thing is his sister is still here and she didn't even know." "That is strange. Why would they let his sister know that he was leaving? Wouldn't he wanted to say goodbye or at least their parents." "Are you sure someone went missing Kirk or are you just messing with us?" "I'm not lying. I'm telling the truth right, Shawn?" "Well." "See you're playing us Kirk and I don't like to be played." "I didn't say that Dani. Let me finish. I'm just not positive that Cash really went missing or not. The counselors did say that he was sent home for bad behavior. And we all know Cash was known for pulling stunts. The thing is Everyone in cabin two said that he went missing because they all went to sleep and the next day he was gone."

"I can't believe this." "What?" "These are the letters that we have been writing home. I wrote this letter a month ago." Danielle said. "You have to be kidding me?" "No, I'm not. I remember this one too. I was telling my parents that I have learned my lesson and I want to come home. Oh, and this one I was telling my parents that I was about to kill Melissa and Kirk." "Hey," Kirk said unamused. "What you get on my nerves." Danielle shrugged her shoulders. "So, this is what you really thought La'Rayna." I looked up and saw that Shawn was reading I guessed what is one of my letters. "I can't be mad, though. You were right." "It's not like I wanted to be right." "Yeah, but you didn't make anything happen either."

"The thing that I am having trouble with is why you keep coming back to this camp Kirk?" "It's not like I knew this was going on." "How can we be so sure. We just met you." "Come on how would I know." "So, you just write letters home year after year and never thought to ask your parents if they received any." "I never write home. My parents don't care about me. They send me to camp to get rid of me." "Not surprised by that," Danielle whispered. I nudged her arm and she mouthed to me what.

It was kind of sad that Kirks parents didn't even care enough about it. It kind of explains why he acts the way he does. He just wants attention because he's not receiving it at home. "Kirk their has to be something else you are not telling us." "Like what?" "I don't know. You are the one that's been coming here every year. You have to remember something. You have to have seen something strange going on." "I told you everything I knew last night."

Hey, whats this?" "A letter duh." Kirk shut up. It looks really old. Like the paper is this brownish yellow color." "Well, what its say?" "Hi, mom today at camp we had a sock hop dance with the boys camp." "Whats a sock hop dance?" "Beats me." "Yeah, this letter is old." Daniele picked up another letter. "Hey look this is from the same girl. It says Mom I really would like to come home. Some strange things have been going on at camp. Everything happened right after the sock hop dance." "What strange things," Kirk said. "Let me finish doofus. Apparently, a kid went missing during the dance. She goes on to say that the camp told everyone that she got sick so they sent her home." "Sounds familiar don't you think?"

"Come on." "Where are we going?" " Have an idea." "Whatever it is I want out of it." "La'Rayna you are the one that wanted answers." "I do but. Just go ahead without me. I want to take a look at this book." "Fine with me. The fewer people the better.

Come on Kirk." "What about me?" "Just stay here for now. This shouldn't take long."

Shawn and Kirk took off to wherever his plan must be. I really wanted to see what this book is about. "So whats up with the book?" "I don't know I haven't looked at it yet." "Do you think it might have some type of clue to whats going on?" "How am I supposed to know?" "Just making conversation." "Okay, Danielle," I said laughing at her. She went back over and started to read through more letters. "Do you think Melissa and Suis know anything." "I don't know maybe." "Well, Melissa ost defneity knows something. I can feel it.Something isn't right with that girl. And the way the other counselors treat her. Ugh, I can't stand her." "Don't we all."

I was flipping through the pages of the book. Nothing out of the ordinary seems to be in here. It looks like some type of journal. Shawn and Kirk came running back into the cabin. "Did you guys find what you need?" "No the place was locked up. But Kirk found a way that we can get in." "Really?" "Yeah until then we need to go back to cabin six. I feel like there is something there we haven't found yet." "Okay, lets go." "No way I'm not going back there." "Come on La'Rayna what happened to the balls you grew yesterday." "How about you come here Kirk and find out." "No, I'm fine right here." "La'Rayna." "No, I'm not going. Besides I want to know what this journal says." "Journal?" "Yes, this book happens to be Jake's journal."

## 21

## CHAPTER 21

I just sat on Shawn's bed looking at the brown book with gold designs on the outside. I was kind of scared to read what Jake had written. What if this journal was a list of who he was going to kill or description of who he has killed. I will never find out if I don't open the book and read it.

Dear, journal

Today is the first day of camp. Truth be told I kind of wish I wasn't here right now. My parents are only making me go because my little sister Melissa really wanted to come. They didn't want her to go alone because she is so young. I don't mine though. Anything for my little sister. I would do anything to make her happy. I can't wait to go home, though. I have a feeling that I will not like it here.

The kids on the bus were pretty annoying. This boy name Tommy was trying to bully a bunch of kids. He actually tried to get the kids to believe that the woods that surround the camp were haunted by a ghost. Who would believe something like that? I just know he better stay away from me and my little sister or we gonna have some problems.

Dear, journal,

It's the second day of camp. My bunks mates are pretty cool. I don't really speak that much to them, though. They have all been coming here since they were my sister's age. Everyone here seems to be best friends. I kind of just hang by myself. Even my little sister has started to make friends. But it's easier at her age, though. Well, it's only day two I have plenty of time to make friends here right?

Dear, journal,

The camp counselor is kind of annoying. We have to sit through these long lectures for a whole week. Who has ever heard of a lecture at camp? We came here to have fun not sit around here to be talked to death.

Some of the staff here are real whack jobs. They give these jobs to anybody now. This one guy name Ted Cutlip or whatever. Hes not much older than me but he is a super goober. I don't know what mental institution they got him out of. I can see him working here for the rest of his life.

Interesting that they still do that boring going over the rules stuff. And Cutlip has been working here since he was a teen. Now, that's just sad. I flipped over some pages to get to the good stuff.

Dear journal,

Camp hasn't been much fun for me. I don't have too many friends here. The only friend that I made went missing a few days ago. Nobody seems to care. Everyone just acts like I'm making it up. They claim nobody with that name was ever at camp. Everybody just makes fun of me and calls me crazy. Saying that I made an imaginary friend. I know I'm not crazy. He was here at this camp. I wasn't the only person that talked or saw him. I just knew something wasn't right about this camp. I don't know what's going on but I'm going to get to the bottom of it.

Reading this I realized Jake was me. I think that's why I had that dream about him. I wonder he ended up finding out about this crazy camp. I can't believe someone went missing all those years as well.

Dear journal,

I wrote my parents a letter telling them to come get me from the crazy camp a week ago. I haven't heard anything back from them. I went to Miss Michelle one of the camp counselors here to ask if I could make a call home. She laughed at me and told me that there are no phones here. She made up so the story about how phones wouldn't work out here because we are so far out in the woods. I asked her how come I haven't heard from my parents. She said it because you have to write to them. After I told her I did she got mad. She frowned at me then smiled and said maybe you try to write them again.

I really don't know whats going on at this camp. Its really starting to scare me. Its like every time I question some of the things that happen here people try to convince me that I'm crazy. I haven't said much to Melissa because shes only a little kid. I don't want to scare. I'm pretty sure she has written to mom and dad. I'll go ask her about it and see if shes heard from them.

Dear journal,

I really miss home. I want to go home so bad that I could just cry. I hate it here. I don't like anybody here and nobody likes me. The only friend I had here went missing and nobody is doing anything about it. Also, I'm starting to think our letters aren't being sent home. I mean why make us right letters home if you aren't even going to send them home in the frist place.

I am really thinking about running away. But I don't want to leave Melissa here by herself. Something isn't right with this place at all. It's not a camp. Maybe if I try and get some information I can prove everyone wrong. I just don't know what to look for.

Dear journal,

Tonight is the night. I'm not the only one who has been feeling this way. We are going to go get some information. I hope our suspicions are right. I have to go now but when I come back everything will be uncovered.

I turned the page and it was blank so I flipped over to another one. That was Jake last entry. I really wondered what he found and how he end up going missing as well. Who was this other person that felt the same way as he did? DId he go off and try to find his friend. DId a killer come and get him.

## 22

**CHAPTER 22**

hey never found his body...now he's hunting everybody...

I was still sitting in Kirk and Shawn cabin. I have no clue what taking them so long. I was looking at some of the letters that were in the bag. I opened one up and there was a picture. The picture was of two little girls smiling and a group of about four boys acting like they were wresting. It was quite comical. The letter read,

Dear mom and dad,

I'm having a great time at camp. These are some of my new friends. We have been hanging out a lot since I got here. We have done all kinds of things like fishing and swiming. Camp fires are my favortive time of the day at camp. We get to roast marshmellows and sing camp songs around the fire. I put a picture of my friends in the letter. If it wasn't for them I don't think I would be enjoying camp. The next to me her name is Melissa. The four boys names are Jake, hes Melissa brother. The other three are his cabin mates. There names are Aden, Jackson, and Jamal. They are really nice. They ind of act like our big brothers. Its nice to have someone looking out for us. Espically after the scary stories they tell us at camp.

Shawns other two bunkmates came back looking for him. I made up some story that Kirk and Shawn were off hiking in the woods. I couldn't say they were anywhere near camp because then they could go look for them and easily see they are nowhere to be found. Those two idiots bought it.

I heard a knock on the door and thought it was strange. Nobody ever knocks on the cabin doors they just come right in unless its night time. Most of the time the doors are open. People walk in and out of them because we all know just about everyone at the camp. I walked over to the door and saw Susie H. I opened the screen door so that she could come in.

"Susie, what are you doing here?" "I've been looking for you and Dani all day. I figured you would be here with Shawn." "Oh, no they aren't here." "Where did they go?" "Uh, Shawn went to go get me an ice pack. My ankle is still a little sore." "Aw, that's too bad. Do you want to go fishing with me by the lake?" Where else would we go fishing? "Uh yeah sure. But I'll kind of want to wait for Shawn to get back." "I'm pretty sure he would spot us at the lake come on." She grabbed my arm basically dragging me out the cabin.

"Susie why are we all the way over here just to go fishing." "Because this is the best fishing spot in the whole camp. There is nobody out here swimming and making a lot of noise. Its easiest for catching something." I looked back at cabin six. We were standing right in front of cabin six. "You don't think it's creepy being out here?" "No, I come out here all the time." "By yourself." "Yeah, why not?" "Is there where you are always disappearing to?" "What do you mean?" She said frowning. "Nevermind." She shrugged her shoulders and continued on fishing. I always knew something was off about Susie but why here?

Danielle, Shawn, and Kirk started to come out cabin six. I tried to make noise to distract Susie from finding out. "Oh look there is a big fish right there," I yelled. "Okay, but you should be quiet maybe we can catch it." I threw my rod in the water letting the wire get tangled with Susie wire. "Oh my bad I didn't mean to, how do I get this out." "Wait La'Rayna don't move so we don't get even more tangled." I started moving more and making more noise.

What are you guys doing over here? "Going fishing?" "By cabin six." "Yes, its the best spot. Hey what are you guys doing over here? I thought you went on a hike?" "We did go on a hike." "The hike trail is on the other side of the lake." "Cool it Susie I was showing them some cool spots up ahead. You've been there." Kirk said. "Yeah and it was no fun. You guys shouldn't have been up there. If you get caught don't say I didn't warn you."

While Susie was busy with the fishing poles We walled off to the side to talk. We know she was still in ear shot so we decided to speak in code. "Did you guys find anything?" "Yeah we found some pretty interesting things. Did you finish reading?" "Um yeah I got through most of it. Not too much information but the story was intresting." "I don't think I'm going to be able to get these poles apart. We might as well head back to camp." "Good idea you lead the way."

We made it back to Shawns and Kirks cabin. We felt like that was th only safe place to discuss things. Susie H went to go put the fishing poles away. Hopefully she goes and finds something else to do like she noramlly does. After we made sure that nobody elsewas going to be borthering us for awhile we started tlking about what we were going to do with the information we found so far.

"Apparently the book was Jakes journal. He wrote an entry about his entire experience at camp. He didn't have any friends and he only came to camp for Melissa sake. He ended up making a friend that went missing as well. He thought creepy and strange stuff was going on at the camp as well. After his friend went missing everyone pretended like the kid never even existed. He never mentioned who this friend was. He was writing letters like we were to our parents but he never heard back from his parents either. His last entry he said that he was going to look for answers."

"What do you think he was looking for?" "I'm not sure. I guess the samething we are." "Do you think he found anything?" "Maybe. It could explain why he went missing." "I bet that was the last time anybody heard from him." "Could be." "So what did you guys find?"

"Well we were never able to get into the cousulers cabin thats why we went back to cabin six. We searched everywhere but couldn't find anything," said Shawn. "But I remember at home sometimes I stuff things I don't want my parents to find under the floorboards." Kirk chimed in. "So we checked under there." "What did you guys find?" "We looked under the floorboards and found a stack of letters. Guess who they are by?" "Jake." "Yeah but these weren't adressed to his parents."

"Did you guys read the letters?" "Well we decide to leave that up to two." "Why us?" "Because we are going back to checkout the couslers cabin. They got to be hiding something in there." "If you guys couldn't get in the first time what makes this time so much different?" "I just have to know what thy are hiding." "Okay do what you have to do but becareful Shawn."

What did Jakes letters say?

"Its the woods. Something has to be out there in the woods. If we can't get into the counsulers cabin we have to go searching in the woods." "No way I'm not going." "We have to thats what Jake did. If he was even close to finding out what happened we have to follow his trail."

"Yeah and look what happened to Jake. We don't even know where his trail started." "Yeah I'm with La'Rayna on this. There aren't enough clues. What are we supposed to go based on assumptions? Whos to say Jake isn't the killer." "You are the one that wanted asnwer la'Rayna." "Yes, I know that. Stop throwing that in my face okay. Look where the answer got us. Nowhere. We haven't found a thing. All we know is that the camp is hiding something and we don't know what exactly. Can't we just leave it at that."

"I'm not willing to. We came so far. What if what we find is exactly what Jake found and it could stop what has been going on at this camp for years." "I feel like we are about to open up a can of worms." "Too late we already did."

We were back here. On these familiar grounds. A place that I never wanted to come again. If we were going to find answer these woods were going to tell us all we needed to know. So we hope. We were walking just passed cabin six.

"What do you expect us to find out here?" "Yeah, I mean we have no clue what Jake was looking for." "I don't plan on looking for what Jake was looking for. We don't have enough information from him to go on." "Well why are we going on this hike?" "To find Cash. Hes got to be around here somewhere. I'm not buying that story the counselors are selling."

**23**

— ⸳ —

## Chapter 23

W hat did Jakes letters say?

Dear Mom and Dad,

Camp has been kind of boring so far. All we are doing so far are going over rules. I'm glad its the last day. The food here isn't too bad but I do miss your cooing mom. If you could send me you famous snickerdoodle cookies I will be set for the whole summer.

Melissa seems to be enjoying camp so far. Shes meeting friends already. I guess it's easy to do that at her age. Don't worry about her though. In really have been looking out for her. I don't know what I would do if anything ever happened to her believe me. I didn't beg for a little sister to see her hurt.

I really do miss you guys and shadow. I can't wait to come home and play with him. Tell him that I miss him and love him. I hope you guys can visit on parents day. The counselors told us that we are supposed to have a parents day later on in the summer. I hope that don't want us to put on some corny play like in The Addam family. I'll write next week. Love you.

Dear mom and dad,

The camp is pretty okay. We do a lot of activities.

My bunkmates are pretty cool. I don't really speak to them like that though. They have been friends since like forever. they all grew up together and been coming to camp every year. There are a lot of fake people here at camp.

People are pretty good at pretending like nothing is wrong. Something isn't right. Its this kid named Tommy who gets away with everything. He is a big bully. He tried to mess with me but I didn't want you told me to dad.

There have been some kids complaining to the camp counselors about him but they don't really do anything regarding him. They think hes a lttle angel. He thinks hes better than everyone because hes dad donates money to the camp. He always gets first dibs on things and the better equipment.

Dear mom and dad,

I wish I could call you guys on the phone so that I know you are actually getting these letters. I'm not sure why you haven't written me back yet. Is because I said that everything is going fine? I just wish that I could hear from you.I hope to see you on parents day in a two months. Tell shadow that I said hi and that I will be home as soon as I can.

Dear mom and dad,

Sorry I haven't been writing every week like I wanted to. But I'm starting to get this feeling like these letters aren't being sent anyways. Its just not like you guys not to respond. Also,

I would like to come home. Can you guys please come and get me. Something strange is going on at the camp. I'm not having any fun here. I haven't even made not one friend. I'm just over this fake camp with all these fake people. This shouldn't be called Camp Lakeview it should be called Camp Fake.

I don't want to be selfish thought because Melissa has made friends and shes having fun. But if shes happy why should I make her sacrifice her fun because of me. I would jsut say come get me and leaver her alone her but I don't want to leave her alone. Not here anyways.

Dear mom and dad,

Today I finally made a friend. I wasn't so sure about him at first but he seems pretty cool. He said he got tired of hanging out with everyone else. he said that he noticed things that I've notced as well. Our bonding didn't have anything to do with the creepy things going at camp. We happened to like a lot of the same thing. Hes like the brother that I never had.

He told me that his parents sent him to camp because he was getting in trouble at home. I know you wouldn't want me to hang out with him. He said that he would do things to get attention at home because hes parents never pay attention to him. Clearly, that didn't work because they just sent him away. I'm glad that I have parents like you guys. I love you.

Dear mom and dad,

I'm starting to have a little fun. My friend and I been hanging out a lot. We went fishing yesterday. He taught me all about fishing. He says that his family has a cabin that they go to ever summer and he learned to fish from his nanny.

Today we plan on going coaneing and maybe go on a hike to catch bugs. Hes into insects too. He wants to become ento-mologist when he grows up. I think thats pretty cool. He can study that while I become a marine biologist.

Also, we started hanging around with his bunkmates and Melissa and her friend. Melissa friend is the sister of his bunk-mates. I kind of like it like this that way I can keep a better eye on her. He bunkmates are pretty okay. We don't hang out that much but when we do its an okay time.

Dear mom and dad,

When I woke up today we all at a serious meeting about staying together and not leaving camp. I searched everywhere for my friend and thats when I realized the meeting was about him. He went missing and nobody knows where he went. A few of the counselors went off to go look for him while the rest of them sayed behind to look after her us.

They made us stay in Mckinley Hall for an entire day. The whole week we had to say in out bunks. It was kind of like we were on lock down. A few kid suck out and got in big trouble for doing so. I really hope hes okay.

Dear mom and dad,

I actually don't even believe you guys are getting these letters but it helps to get everything off my chest. Afterall of these strange things thats been happening at camp I wouldn't be surprised. My friend was never found. They acted as if he never went missing. First they daid that he was sent home for bad behavoir. Now they are telling me he never even exist.

I don;t really know whats going on here but I know I'm not crazy. Thats what everyone seems to thin. I really just want to get Melissa and myself out of here. I have to go find answer. I'm putting a picture of us indie this letter to give you guys proof that he was here with me at camp. I love you guys.

**24**

— · —

## Chapter 24

"What do you expect us to find out here?" "Yeah, I mean we have no clue what Jake was looking for." "I don't plan on looking for what Jake was looking for. We don't have enough information from him to go on." "Well, why are we going on this hike?" "To find Cash. He's got to be around here somewhere. I'm not buying that story the counselors are selling."

Shawn was right. I don't believe anything they are telling us either but what makes him think that finding him will lead to any answers. And besides, how will we find him. "Well, how do you plan on doing that?" "Thats why we are going on this hike." "IF they couldn't find him what makes you think that we will? Finding him what is that going to do?" "I don't know but I can't sit around and do nothing."

We have been walking in the woods for over an hour now. And there was still no sign of Cash. I'm not even sure if he is actually in these woods. But whos blood could that have been on the back of Jakes journal? I sometimes think that maybe we should've handed that to the police or something. They could've at least took DNA from it or something. What are we getting ourselves into?

Danielle and Kirk were up some ways covering different angles that Shawn and I weren't. Kirk thought that it would be a brilliant idea to split up that way we could cover more ground but Shawn wasn't so trusting in that. What if one of us ends up missing as well. He thought it would be easier for us to just cover different areas of the woods while trailing each other. That way none of us would get lost and in case something happened we would all be together.

"Shawn, do you really believe he's out here?" "Who knows. That why we are out here trying to find out." "So you think that he is out here somewhere. Like alive?" "I'm not sure." The look on his face told a different story than the one in his voice. Its like he really wanted to believe that Cash was still alive but he knew that he wasn't.

Over the past few months at camp, we grew to know more and more of the other campers. Cash is one of them. He was a really cool dude that liked to joke around all the time. He always put a smile on my face. It was like he didn't want to see anybody sad. His sister was the cutest and sweetest little girls ever. And you could tell that he was very protective of her.

Shawn grew close to him as well. I guess that's why he wants to find him so bad. The thing is I'm not so sure that finding him will lead us to any answers.

"It's getting dark can we do this tomorrow?" "La'Rayna don't be such a scary cat." "I don't get why we have to do this at night. If Cash went missing what do you think can happen to us at night." "I won't let anything happen to you alright but we have to do this. Its either now or never." "Yeah, we may never get another chance. Right now everyone is at the campfire." "Yep and since its so many of us they aren't thinking about three people missing at the campfire right now." "So, are you with us or not." "Fine. Where do we start?"

It either now or never. I'm so sick of hearing that. I just want to go home and get off this camp not look for more trouble. I just have a really bad feeling about everything. Like something bad is going to happen. You know in those horror movies when a group of kids goes looking for answers but all they find are cryptic information and then end up dead. Yep just like that. I don't want that happening. I know its just a movie but still, you never know.

"There just has to be something that we are missing." "What could we possibly be missing? We don't know what's going on." "Yeah we looked in cabin six, we read Jake journal, and we never got into the counselors cabin." "I don't know I just have a feeling like we are missing something."

"Well, you read Jakes journal so you know more about him." "What that doesn't make sense. I already told you his journal didn't really say anything." "Well, what about the letters." "The same as the journal." "Wait." "What is it?" "You guys found those letters under the floorboards of cabin six right?" "Yeah so." "Well, back then the cabins were numbered different from the boys to the girls. And cabin six was an active cabin back then." "Okay, I don't see where you are going with this." "Cabin six had to be the cabin that Jake stayed at years ago. Just think about it."

"That's impossible the cabin was supposed to be closed down years ago." "How did Jakes letters get under the floorboards in cabin six and his journal in the closest?" "Yeah, and why was there blood on the back of the journal?" "Well I don't know how the blood got there but that does make sense. Something isn't adding up." "None of this is adding up." "And we haven't gotten down to the bottom of nowhere."

"So, I don't see the point in this let's just turn back around while we can." "Not going to happen." "I know La'Rayne we have come too far to go back now. It's either now or never. Do you want to know the truth or not." "I do but." "There are no buts its just a yes." I do but how will any of this lead us to the truth? What is this truth that we are looking for?

"Does anybody have any ideas?" "Maybe he put the letters under the floorboards to give the next person clues to what happened." "I mean I guess. I never read those." "Why not?" "I only got to the letters that were addressed to his parents. The other letters weren't addressed to anybody. I thought it was maybe more parts of his journal or something. The journal didn't give any clues and I got tired of reading about this gut feeling that he never elaborated about. I do admit it was the same gut feeling that I was having but gut feelings don't give answers."

"Well, where are the letters now?" "I left them back at the camp. The letters are not going to help us out here." "Shes right we came out here to find Cash nothing more and nothing less. We can take a look at the letters when we get back. Right now we need to find Cash before it gets dark out." "By the looks of it we need to get going."

"Well if Cash is out here I feel like the first place he would be is in the cave." "The cave?" Yeah, remember the cave I took you guys to a month back?" "See now we are getting somewhere." "Looks like you have a brain after all Kirk." "Dani don't start." "What?" "You know what." "As I was saying. the cave is the perfect spot if Cash was still out here alive. If he was lost and couldn't find his way back that is where he would be. Its perfect for shelter." "Yeah, your right lets go."

"Hey, look I found something." We heard Kirk up ahead shout. "What is it?" "I don't know its covered in mud. We rushed up ahead to meet Kirk and Danielle." Kirk was bent down pulling whatever he found up. "It...its a jacket." "Do you think it may have been Cash jacket?" "Really likes he's been surviving out here all by himself on his own." "Do you think he's been out here on his own?" "How redundant." "Thank you" "Figures you wouldn't get it." "What?" "Guys we really don't have time to hear you guys argue right now. It's getting dark out. We need to do what we came here to do and leave. Now Kirk where is this cave at again?" "Its not too far from here. Come on lets go."

We continued walking along the trail until Kirk led us off the path. I don't remember going this way last time but then again I don't know where the cave is at in the first place so who am I to question.

"Whoa, whats that smell? It's almost similar to the smell in cabin six." "Gross you're right." "Where could it be coming from." "Maybe it's a dead animal or something." "Or a dead body," Kirk stated. "Don't start butthead," Danielle said. He stretched his arms out towards Danielle and started to make scary noises. "I'm going to get you, Danielle." "Cut it out before I make you." She held up her fist towards him." "Yeah Kirk we didn't come here for games," Shawn said. "Alright geesh I'm sorry. Only trying to lighten up the mood."

As we got closer to the cave the smell just seemed to get more and more unbearable. We trailed the cave because Shawn wanted to make sure that it was safe before we entered. It was now dark outside causing the cave to be pitched black so I understood his caution. We walked inside the cave behind Shawn.

"Hey, Kirk how far back did you say this cave goes?" "I'm not sure but I heard that there is a tunnel in here somewhere that leads to a rode." "This place is huge." "If Cash is in here he could be anywhere then." "Should we split up." "That's what someone always says before someone ends up dead." "No, weren't not going to split up I don't see the point. Just spread out some you guys are too close to me." He was right we were practically sqeezing behind Shawn like we were afaird." "Yeah back up guys," said Kirk clearing his throat. "Boy calm down you are the main one holding on to my arm for dear life," Danielle said back to him.

Not trying to hear them bicker again I decided to look for something that could lead us to Cash. We found his jacket outside so he must have left it and came in here to keep warm. But what could have frightened him so bad to leave his jacket outside? I heard some noise towards the right of the cave so I started to walk that way. I pointed the flashlight to the back. "Uh." I said to myself. I tried to look at the back but the light didn't carry that far.  In order for me to see what that was I decide to walk closer.

"Ow." I tripped over something. "Are you okay?" "Yes, Man why am I the one always falling." "Because you're clumsy." "Shut up Kirk." I dusted my pants off and Shawn came over to help me up. I stood up to look for my flashlight. Once I found it on the ground I lean down to pick it up. I felt something wet as I picked up my flashlight. "Uh, whats this?" I whispered to myself. "Whats wrong?" Shawn asked. I didn't say anything I just flashed my flashlight on my hands. They were red. Please don't tell me this is blood again. "La'Rayna your hands," Shawn said grabbing them. Danielle and Kirk walked over towards us. I flashed my flashlight in the direction that I felt the wet substance wanting to know what it was and where it came from. "Is that is that a body?"

The camp has been on a lockdown since we discovered the body. We have only been allowed to leave our cabin to go to the dining hall and that's about it. They were thinking about closing the camp down and sending us all home. The owner came to check things out. He told them no because he didn't want to scare the families or the other campers.

We are the only four that knows what really is going on. The counselors and the owner of the camp held a meeting and lied. They told everyone here that there was an animal lose and for our safety, it was best if we go on a lockdown. He ensured that there was nothing to be worried about and that everything is under control. He even had fake people come out like they were animal control. Who knows if they called the police.

"Ugh I'm so sick of being stuck in this cabin," said Danielle. "Well try being stuck in here with you," said Melissa. Danielle glared at her. "You know what I'm sick of your mouth." "Not as I am sick of your face." "Why don't you try to look in the mirror." "Oh, I have all the time actually and it's quite lovely." "Let's see how lovely you will look with a black eye." "I'll like to see you try." They bickered back and forth.

"Guys enough already." "Well, she started it." "I don't care who started it. Its bad enough that we have to sit in here all day." Danielle rolled her eyes at Melissa and plopped down on her bed. Melissa sat back on her bed and pulled out a magazine. "I swear I can't stand her," Danielle mumbled.

"Hey, I know how about we play a game." Susie H said. "Yeah you go hide and we don't look." Melissa starting again. "Don't start that mess again." "It's okay." "No, it's not okay. Don't let her talk to you like that. Don't let anybody talk to you like that." "So, what game do you want to play?"

We played a few quiet games. One because there isn't much we can really do in this cabin and two we didn't want to hear Melissa's mouth again. As long as she minds her business and we mind ours I say that its a nice day.

"Don't cheat while I'm in the bathroom." "Cheat you are the one that cheated last game." I yelled at Danielle as she went to the bathroom." I looked up and Melissa wasn't sitting on her bed. I hope they don't get to arguing in there. Danielle came out rubbing her eyes and yawning. "Where did Melissa go?" She spoke. "Uh?" "I said Where did Melissa go?" "I thought she was in the bathroom with you." "Oh, I think she left." Susie H said casually. "What do you mean shes left?" "I saw her leave when we playing Uno." "That was two games ago and we are on a locked down nobody is supposed to leave the cabins."

Melissa's privilege has always bothered me. Her reasoning for coming back, her brothers' disappearance, and the way she acts just doesn't add up. One child goes missing yet you send the other one back to camp. On top of all that she always seems to disappear when something happens.

I've been trying to put all of the clues together. I don't believe that Jake is the so-called camp killer. His disappearance and suspicion of the camp contradict that. When I had that dream about him and found his bracelet was so that I could find the connection. So, what am I missing? I got it.

"Danielle we have to get out of here." "What we are on locked down we can't leave." "But we have to get to Shawn's cabin I think I figured it out. Maybe not the whole truth but part of it. "I know a way out." We both turned to look at Susie H. "Look I know I don't agree with you guys leaving but I haven't been blind to what you guys have been doing this whole time." "What are you talking about?" "I may look like a ditsy person but I only act that way so people wouldn't get suspicious of me."

"You know you saying that doesn't really help." "I mean so people would notice that I know certain things about them. See, look I've been coming here for a few years now and every time I had to bunk with Melissa and never liked her attitude. When I found out what happened to her brother I thought it was strange as well that she keeps coming back. And shes very bratty yet none of the counselors do anything about it." "What does this have to do with anything?" "You mean you guys don't know." "Know what?"

"I overheard you guys one day talking about finding out what the camp has been hiding so I started following Melissa around to help." "So, what did you find out?" "Unfortainly not a thing. I just notice when she randomly disappears. when things happen" "That doesn't really help." "Yeah but she's right I noticed that too." "Sorry, if it doesn't but if you guys want to get out of here I can show you how." "Lead the way."

She lead us over to the back door. She bends down and started to pick at the silver sheet that was on the door. "You see this. This right here is covering up a hole in the door. All you have to do is take this out lift the sheet up and boomed a way out." She was right there was a hole right in the door. The whole wasn't small but it wasn't that big either. We would have to squeeze our way out. But at least it was a way out.

# 25

## CHAPTER 25

We were all sitting around the nightly lit campfire that we have each night before we head to our cabins for the rest of the night. I don't know what made them want to lift the lock-in. I certainly didn't feel safe being out here. I really just wanted to go home at this point.

"Guys, do you really think its safe to be out here? I mean this camp is crazy." "Yeah I agree with Danielle," I said. "Why would the camp let us came back out here if it wasn't." "Because we just found a body in the woods you big dumb jerk." I semi-yelled at Kirk. "La'Ranya calm down," Shawn said looking around. "Nobody knows that but us. They lied to the campers and the police. At least we know this much about whats really going on here." "Yeah but we already knew the consuolers were lairs." "Yeah but now we know that Cash wasn't sent home.

This much is true. That was the scary part. They lied and told us that they sent Cash home because of bad behavior but this whole time he was out there in the woods dead. If I wanted to go home before I really wanted to get out of here now.

After seeing Cash body laying there on the ground I became numb. I was too scared to move. I guess that was where the blood came from that was on the back of Jakes journal. Question is how did is blood get on Jake Journal.

"Yeah so again is it safe for us to be out here right now," Danielle said. "If the police didn't see anything wrong I guess it is." "Yeah, maybe it was just an accident. Maybe we are overreacting to this whole thing" said Kirk. "I agree. Maybe we are trying to find something that's not there. We never found any real evidence. We should just let it go." "I guess. Maybe thats why they haven't said anything because they don't want to scare anybody."

"That's all I really want. That and to get out of this camp." I whispered to myself." "Rayna are you sure?" "Yes, I sick of this. We haven't gotten anywhere and I'm tired of being scared. You guys are right maybe we just made it all up. Maybe we wanted to believe that something was going on." "But we did prove that." "Yeah, I guess but I just. I don't know. All I know is that Cash is dead and we found nothing."

Shawn looked at me with so much sorrow. Like he was hurt because I was hurting, I didn't want to feel this way anymore. We should just drop this whole thing. There are only a few more weeks left of camp. Maybe if we can just forget about it and stop looking for answers everything will go back to normal and we can go home in peace.

"So we all agree. To give up and move on." "Yeah, we only have a few more weeks of camp left. No point in running around paranoid." "Okay then. Nothing happened and the body we found wasn't Cash. It was just an accident gone wrong." "Yeah and accdednt gone wrong." We agreed.

That was the best thing that we thought at the time. We weren't sure what was going on and we didn't have any answers. We are only kids. There's nothing more that we can do. The only things we were going based on were our gut feelings and Jakes journal. We didn't bother to look at those letters when we reach camp. We ran straight towards the camp office to explain what we saw. Whatever answer we were looking for will just get buried with those letters.

"I think that I'm just going to head back to the cabin." "Are you sure?" "Yeah, I don't feel like being out here right now." "Want me to walk with you." "No, I'll be fine." "Are you sure." "Yes, Shawn I'll be fine." "Wait up La'Rayna I'll go with you. I don't feel like being out here anymore either." "I guess I'll head on back as well. I'll see you guys tomorrow." Shawn hugged us both and headed in the opposite direction to the boy's cabins with Kirk.

We were back in our cabins. The campfire was still going on. It tends to last longer on Friday nights. After being on lockdown they decided to extend it even longer. But we decided to call it a night. I was just exhausted after everything that has been going on lately. Even though we agreed to forget about it I just couldn't shake the feeling that something bad was going to happen. It was just too soon.

Maybe going over Jakes letter wouldn't be a bad idea. I know I want to forget but those letters just keep toughing on the back of my mind. I got up and went into my drawe to pull them out. I didn't want to read the letters by myself this time. It was best if we all took a look to see what they meant.

"Danielle are you still up?" "Yeah, why?" "I know we said that we will forget it but I can't." "I understand because I can't stop thinking about it." "I know." "It's just that Cash body lying in that cave. I keep seeing that over and over. What if that was us? And how can we forget something like that La'Rayna how could we?" "I don't know." "That was no accident someone had to do that to him. What if they are still out there." "I know Danielle we have to go talk to Shawn." "Well, what are we waiting for? Let's go."

In Shawns cabin

"Come on guys I thought we were giving that stuff up." "We were but something isn't sitting right with me." "Yeah and I'm going to side with Rayna on this one. We found a body in the woods and nobody did a thing about it. Doesn't that frighten you." "Okay, so what are we supposed to do we didn't find anything. Where do we start." "Kirk was there years ago."

"Uh," Kirk said while stuffing marshmallows down his throat. "Kirk you don't remember anything about the year Melissa brother went missing I mean you were there." "Yeah, but I was only five. I don't remember that." "Can you think of something I mean there is a brain in there right?" Danielle said. "Guys seriously it's not the time to argue."

"Shawns right. And I have a really bad feeling somethings going to happen." "Where do we start then?" "Jakes letters. The ones we found in cabin six." "My only problem with that is how did his letters end up in cabin six in the first place. Wasn't that cabin supposed to be closed down for years?" "The camp opened in the 1970s. The cabins were labeled differently. Years ago when Melissa was five her brother went missing because he was going to look for his friend. The camp covered the story up. Whats going on now is the exact same thing that happened to Jake years ago." Kirk stated. "How do you know this?" "The song."

Danielle and I headed back to our cabin. There was nothing more that we could do. Jakes letters explained it all. I just can't believe all of that was going on. None of it didn't explain his disappearance. But could Jake be the killer? Could he be the reason why people have been gone missing? If he was I could understand why. It certainly explains Melissa situation. But there's no evidence point to him. Maybe it was just a warning.

"Rayna." "Yes." "What do you think is going to happen?" "I'm not sure." She took a deep breath. "Look, I just want to say that if anything happens." I could sense that she was preparing to tell me a be safe goodbye type speech. "No, don't say that." "But I just want." "Danielle I know I have a bad feeling about everything but I don't know. Maybe its all in my head." "What about Cash and the letters." "I understand that but." I didn't even have to finish she understood. "Yeah well, I'm going to shower." "Yeah me too a hot one." "Most defetily."

After our shower, we both just laid in bed. I was reading a book called the 'Let the Circle be Unbroken'  while Danielle flips through pages of her fashion magazine. I was reading but I really wasn't reading. I get what Danielle was saying before and I don't blame her because I still have those same feelings. I just want them to go away. I just want to go home.

"Only a few more weeks left. it's going to be alright." I'm guessing she could sense my uneasiness. "I know I'm just ready to leave now." "We can't do anything about that. Do you want me to go get Shawn." "Yes please." Anytime I was feeling down Shawn was the only one that could make me feel better.

Danielle came back in with Shawn and Kirk. Who knows why Kirk decided to follow along. "La'Rayna are you okay?" "I just want to go home." He took his hand to move some hair out of my face. "It's going to be alright okay. We only have a few weeks left of camp and then we can go home." "I don't know I just feel like something bad is going to happen." He looked at me with wide eyes then hugged me. "I'm not going to let anything happen to you. I can promise you that." He whispered in my ear. "I promise you."

There was a loud crash like glass being broken then we heard screams. "Oh, my gosh what was that?" "You both stay here I'll go check it out." "Shawn no." I grabbed his arm. "I'll be alright. Come on Kirk." Shawn and Kirk headed out the cabin while Danielle and I stayed behind. "Skip this I'm going to see whats going on."

I followed Danielle out of the cabin in the direction of where Shawn and Kirk went. Back to where the campfire was being held. I saw Shawn bend down and Kirk was walking around in a circle. "Shawn" I called out. His head snapped up in my direction. "What are you guys doing here I thought I told you to stay in the cabin. "What is going on?" "Oh my gosh." I heard Danielle say.

"Whats going on." I walked closer to her. "No, No don't go over there." Shawn tried to grab my arm but it was too late I had already seen what happened. "Oh my gosh, Oh my gosh." There were three bodies lying next to the campfire. "Are they dead?" "Looks like it."

There was an announcement that rang throughout the camp telling us all to go back inside our cabins and to keep the doors locked. "This is an emergency. We need all the campers to please return to your cabin and lock all the doors. Your counselors will be doing rounds making sure you are all safe inside. We will give you more information once you are all accounted for."

"What is going on?" "Come on lets go." Shawn grabbed my arm and pushed us to leave. "Shawn." "We have to get out of here." "So you are taking us back to the cabins." "Yes, just go back to your cabin grab somethings and wait until I come to get you." "Well, what about what they said over the announcements." "Forget about what they said Kirk. Look at what happened. people are dead. I'm sick of listening to what this camp has to say." "Danielle is right Kirk. That's why I say we need to leave soon. Just go back to the cabin. Do as they say and wait until I come and get you guys."

We rushed back to our cabins. As soon as we step foot on the steps I heard a loud scream coming from the far left cabin. For some reason, I froze in my spot. I turned my head in the direction of the scream but saw nothing but black. The sky has gotten darker. "La'Rayna come on." Danielle grabbed my hand pulled me inside the cabin. Once we reached inside we slammed the door shut an locked it.

I looked around and notice that both Susie H and Melissa was missing. I went over and grabbed my backpack and put a few items in there. Now, all we have to do is wait for Shawn. There was a knock on the door causes me to jump. "Its okay maybe its one of the couslers. You know they are supposed to do a check." "Danielle what if its a killer." "La'Rayna." "No don't open the door." I have seen too many horror movies to even think about opening the door. The knock came again followed by a voice. "Come on guys let me in." "See its Susie I'm going to open it."

When Danielle opened the door Suis came in following Melissa behind her. "Why did you guys lock the door." "Didn't you hear the announcement." "Yeah but we weren't in here yet. What are you guys trying to do uh lock us out and hope that we die" Melissa said? "We couldn't be so lucky."

"Where were you guys anyway?" "Is that any of your business." "there may be a killer lose and you guys are just prancing in here after all this time." "if I was the killer you would've been dead." "oh is that a threat." "you would know if it was." "Come on guys calm down we were still at the campfire. Something happened so they took us to Mckinly hall." "What happened?" "We don't know. We heard screaming and the rounded those who were left at the campfire into Mckinly hall and told us to wait inside. After that, the announcement came on telling us all to get back into the cabins."

Danielle and Melissa started fighting. It was really aggravating because something serious is going on and all these two can do is argue with each other. I get why Danielle said something to Melissa because shes always starting something but now is not the time. Maybe its her way into getting Melissa to slip up and say something. I just know that I'm sick of the bickering.

"Come on guys stop fighting something scary is going on here and fighting isn't going to help." "Yeah neither is staying here," Melissa said. "So, what are you saying?" "I'm getting out of here." "You can't go." "Yeah right I can. I'm not waiting to be killed." "We don't know if there is a killer or not. Besides what if counselor Sarah comes and we aren't here?" "Who cares I'm out."

Melissa begins packing stuffing things into her pack. She does have a point. Why sit around and wait to be killed. It's not like we were staying ourselves so no sense in trying to stop her. We couldn't let Susie stay here either. I just have to convince her to come with us. The announcement rang through the camp again. "Everyone should be in their cabin by now in a few minutes your camp counselors will be there in a minute to check on you and explain what to do next. We ask everyone to remain calm and to not leave their cabin."

We heard someone screaming at first but we thought it was just because of the ghost stories. People are always getting scared of the stories because some of them are to be true. But that scream was different it was as if someone was dying.

**26**

—— ◆ ——

## CHAPTER 26

We looked out the window and seem something coming out the cabin across from ours and something spotted us. We started to run toward the back of the cabin and sneak out the back way. If Susie never showed us this we would've had a way out. "Hurry up." "Get it open." For some reason, Susie was struggling to lift the metal part off the door. I guess she was scared and panicking. Danielle pushed her out the way and got it up. She looked up at the both of us. "Go." Susie went first then it was my turn.

"Danielle help me my foot stuck." She rushed back over to pull my foot out. Then the door slammed open and there it was standing there. "Come on La'Rayna pull harder." "I'm trying." I finally got my foot unstuck and we headed towards the back door but it wouldn't open. "La'Rayna climbed through the whole." "But Danielle." I didn't want to leave her and she knew it but it was the only way. "Just do it you're the smallest you will fit and then I'll go it will be faster that way." I did as she said and reached my hand in to help her out.

As she grabbed on to my hand that's when it grabbed onto her. "Uhhh let me go." "Danielle I got you don't let go," I said pulling her harder. "Please let go." She looked at me with pleading eyes and that's when I knew she wasn't talking about it and begging him to let her go she was talking to me. I shook my head at her. "No Danielle I got you I will not let you go." I knew I wasn't strong enough but I just couldn't leave her there she didn't leave me. She looked at me one last time his grip was too strong and I lost hold of her. "Uhhhh." "DANIELLE NOOOOO!" I shouted.

How could I let her go? I lie there and watch as he smiled at her than me like this was some kind of game that he was getting ready to play and enjoy because he won. She screamed trying to kick it off her. "Danielle I'm coming," I said while I tried to wiggle my way back in. "No run don't worry about me." She continues to kick until it stabbed her in her stomach. He did it over and over again while she screamed at the top of her lungs and all I could do is sit there and watch. There was so much blood everywhere. I was helpless she was helpless and I couldn't even help her. I was in shock I couldn't move

"Danielle." I was frozen and I couldn't move. All I saw was blood. Blood was everywhere. I just stood there watching Danielle be stabbed to death. I couldn't do anything but watch my best friend die. I felt a tug on my arm but my feet stayed planted. "La'Rayna come on we have to go." Susie's voice rang in my ears. She pulled on my arm harder lifted my feet off the ground. I turned around and ran right alongside her hoping to get away.

I felt so guilty leaving Danielle behind. But what could I do? "Susie where are we going." "I don't know but we have to get far away as we can." "We have to hide." "Come on I know a place in the woods. If we can just make it there we should be fine." "The woods." "Yeah."

The woods was the last place that I wanted to be right now. After finding Cash body in the cave and knowing that anybody who runs into the woods gets killed. I wanted to go somewhere that wasn't by the camp. But this camp is surrounding by woods. When I thought that we were far enough from the cabin I stopped in my track to take a breather.

"Come on we have to keep going." "I have to find Shawn first. I can't leave him." "If he isn't dead I'm pretty sure he's long gone." When she said that I pretty much lost it. "No, no he isn't he wouldn't leave me. He might be out there looking for me." Tears started to fall from my face uncontrollably. That's when it hit me that Danielle really is dead. Shes not behind me. Shes not catching up. Shes never coming back. "La'Rayna it isn't your fault." "She died because of me." "No, she died because there is a crazy person out there killing people. You can't blame yourself for that."

We heard someone screaming and I wasn't about to think twice I ran into the closest place I knew to hide. I couldn't tell how far the scream was but I wasn't about to wait to find out.

The old bathhouse had to be the closest place. The bathhouse of all places. Who knows what could be hiding in here. This place hasn't been in use for a few years now. The good thing is there was more than one way to get out. "La'Rayna wait up." I hear Susie whisper.

I slowly walked in there trying not to be heard and while keeping my eyes open to anything else here. I felt something bump into so I jumped. When I turned around I realize that it was just Susie. "Sorry." "Not so close. And try not to make so much noise." Once we made it to the other side of the showers I hid in...keeping watch for anything coming and going.

"Do you think its safe to go out yet?" "I don't know let me go ask the killer if its safe to come out?" I didn't mean to be so rude to her. I have never been rude to her. Like I stated before I get defensive when I'm scared. "I'm sorry." "Its okay I understand." "Let's just go I know we can't stay in here forever. We have to keep moving."

When I was sure that there wasn't anymore screaming for while we left out of the bathhouse. "La'Rayna where are you going?" "I'm going to go look for Shawn." "Are you cray there is a killer on the lose." "Don't you think I know that." "Yeah but." "But nothing I'm not leaving him out here." "What if hes already dead?" "Don't say that." "I'm just being realistic here. He could already be dead if not he may have already left who knows." "I know that I'm not leaving him. If he is alive I'm going to find him and we both are getting off this camp." "I can't. I can't come with you. I'm sorry I just can't." "I don't expect you to."

Her eyes were more frightened than mines. I don't know if it was the determination in me to find Shawn or me going off alone. I didn't expect her to come with me nor did I want her to. We gave each other a hug because we went our separate ways. "Be careful La'Rayna." "I will you too." "I mean it now. You were actually someone for the first time to call a friend." "Thank you." With that, we took off in different directions not knowing if we would ever see each other again.

After I saw Susie red curly hair bounce off into the woods I turned to leave. I was walking slowly trying not to make any noise. I was creeping behind anything that I could hide behind whenever I hear a noise nearby. Luckily it has only been small animals like rabbits and squirrels. I really didn't want to leave Susie but I couldn't leave Shawn behind. Not after what happened to Danielle. I'm not trying to lose another friend.

I stopped in my tracks because I heard someone talking. They didn't sound like the killer. I'm pretty sure it was the killer because who and why would he be talking to anybody. I listened closer and the person sounded like Shawn. I kept following the sound of his voice until I was right in front of him. He was sitting on the ground next to a body. I couldn't make out who it was.

"Shawn." my voice came out shaky. His head snapped in my directions. He got up and practically tackled me to the ground.

"I'm so glad that you are alright." "Me too." I hugged him tightly. He pulled back and looked at me. His eyes are full of so much love and remorse. Then he looked behind me. "Wheres Danielle is she behind you?" "Shawn." My voice cracked. "Shes shes is gone." I started breaking down crying. He pulled me into another hug.

"Shawn I'm so sorry," I said into his shoulder. "For what?" "Not helping Danielle." "Rayna its not your fault." "It is its all my fault. We told me to leave and I should've stayed to help her." "Look and me and listen if there was anything that you could've done she would have never told you to leave." I looked back catching a glance of who was laying on the ground. It was one of Kirks echos.

"What happened to him?" "We were in our cabin when we heard screaming. Kirk and I thought it was more people by the campfire or something. But since we knew what we saw we locked the cabin door to what for Cpulser Mike to come and check on us like they announced. We heard knocking on the door but we were both too afraid to open the door. The knocking came again and then counselor Mikes voice rang through so we opened the door. His voice trailed off and he looked back at Josh.

"What happened. Shawn?" "It wasn't counselor Mike. He came in. He caught Josh as we ran to the back of the cabin. Henry tried to help him. He killed Henry and he grabbed Kirk and Kyle and took them somewhere." "Where?" "I'm not sure we are the only two that got away. I went to your cabin but saw the door was wide open and figure you guys left or something. And he's hurt so we didn't make it far." "Is he going to be alright?" "I'm not sure."

"We can't stand here out in the open we have to hide." "Can you walk?" "Yeah, it just hurts." The closest thing to us was the counselor's bunk. I'm pretty sure its locked like always but we have to try something. "Maybe we can hide in there." "I already check that it's locked." The screaming started up again and this time it was dangerously close. "Well, we can hide by there. We have to do something we can't stay out in the open."

We help Josh off the ground and onto his feet. We slowly walked to the bunk. There was bushes on the right side of the bun so we hid behind that. We his right in time. "Ohmy gosh." I whispered. I covered my mouth hoping that I wasn't heard. I just couldn't believe what I was seeing.

"Help, Help is!" Two people came staggering out into the open. How could they think they would get any help out in the open yelling like that. One was already covered in blood. I don't think that I knew them because I didn't recognize who they were. The one covered in blood fell to the ground. "Carter!" The girl screamed. She ran over to him "Please get up." She begged crying. The thing I know the killer came behind her and cut her throat. Carter, I guess tried to get up but was stabbed right back down.

There was a loud scream coming from another direction. I could see the someone far away runoff. They must have seen what we did. The killer caught them as well because he ran after them. Josh looked like he was ready to pass out. "Whats wrong with him?" "I don't know might be an infection. I need you to do something for me." "What is it?" "I need you to run." "What?" "I need you to run and get away from here." "I'm not leaving you." "Rayna it's not an option." "What about you and Josh?" "We will be fine. I'm going to go try and find some medinece or something. And Kirk." "Shawn." "Just listen to me okay. You being safe means more to me than anything. I promise I'll catch up." "Promise?" "I do. Rayna whatever you do don't stop running." "What about you?" "Don't worry about me just keep running?" But Shawn." "Just keep running I'll be okay promise me you will keep running." "I promise."

I was running and I couldn't stop. If I did I would be dead right now. I wanted to go back for Shawn but he made me promise not to. I really didn't want to leave him and I hope he's okay. I can't lose another friend.

I tried to shake the image of my best friend being murder. But I couldn't it was still playing in my head over and over reminding me that I could be next. It was my fault that she's dead now. She was trying to save me. I was almost caught. I said I wouldn't peek out but something was telling me to. Then I heard someone calling for help. I knew who it was so I climbed put to help them.

"Uhhh." I heard screaming I hope that wasn't Shawn. I don't know what I would do if I lost him too. Oh, my gosh Danielle. The screaming started again. I dived right behind a bush when I heard someone rustling in the woods. I peeked out to see if anyone was there but not too much because I didn't want him or her to see me. I wasn't stupid and I wasn't going to call out and ask who was there. I started to shake and I didn't know if it was because it was freezing cold out or if it was because how scared I am. I wonder if everyone at camp is okay. Well for the people that are still alive.

I can't believe this is all happening. One minute we are having a campfire and the next thing you know we are all being hunted down by a crazy killer. I just knew something bad was going to happen. I'm so scared I don't know what to do. I can't stop crying. I can't believe Danielle is gone. My best friend is dead and I don't know what happened to Shawn. He told me to stay and wait for him. He said he would be back but he never came. I was still sitting in the bush until I heard a noise. I tried to stay quiet but I had to act or I probably would be dead by now.

I'm just too scared to leave. What if the killer gets me. But if I stay here I'm dead for sure. I heard someone calling for help. I knew who it was so I climbed out to help them. They started to stagger towards me. I reached my arm out to grab there hand. She just reached the tip of my fingers. I got a glimpse of her now dark blue eyes. They used to be bright as the sky. She locked eyes with mines then froze and fell face down in the ground. I jumped back and screamed when I saw the knife in her back. "Oh no Susie H."

I tried to get out. No words left my mouth. I knew I had to get out of there. Whatever or whoever must have heard my screams. I dash all the while hiding behind a tree after tree to take a breather and so I wouldn't be seen. I made it to McKinley Dining Hall. The place where we sat and ate, telling stories from our day earlier at camp, and just simply goofing off.

I looked across the empty room just thinking how we will never get a chance to do it again. It's not like the room was the same anyways there was blood everywhere. I heard a loud crash outside and ran straight to the back to hide. Once I reach the back where she was laying faced down covered in blood. I fell to my knees in front of her and picked up her necklace.

Amelia. Although she was a camp counselor that still didn't make the site of her death easy. We all knew they were hiding something from us so its not a shock that she would be dead. Its just sad you know. Because she was one of the nicest cousloers out of them all. She started working here two years ago so it wasn't her fault. I'm sure she knew what happened.

Kind of like the story of Jason. if you don't do anything about it the situation you are part of the problem. Bad things have been going on at this camp for years and nobody did a thing about it. I'm not excusing the killer because what hes doing still doesn't make any of this right.

I hear rustling around out in the hall. This isn't really a great place to hide. There is no way out. I slowly got up and climbed over her body. I crawled further to the back and hid behind some shelves. I pulled my knees up to my chest and begin to pray silently. Please please please go away.

"Hello is anybody in here." I heard someone whispered. For all that I know it could be the voice of the killer. I didn't move an inch. My breathing slowed and I just hoped whoever it was would just leave. I heard more movement and it sounds like the person is getting closer to me. Please please, please. I kept my eyes steady so I could see whoever it was. They spoke again.

"Oh my gosh." They whispered again. I'm guessing they found the body. The door to the place slammed shut. There was light shuffling and I saw a shadow sit down across from the shelves that I was hiding behind. I guess they weren't the killer. I tried to make out who it was but all I saw was eyes looking back at me. Their eyes widen. Whoever it was lifted their finger up to their lips letting me know to be quiet. Who am I a fool, of course, I'm going to be quiet.

The back door swung opened and I heard a thud sounding as if someone hit the floor. Feet running passed me and another pair slowing going by. "No, please don't please." I could hear them begging for their life. I so wanted to get out and help but what could I do. I couldn't even help Danielle. The screams of the person were just unbearable. I covered my ears and squeezed my eyes shut. There was nothing like hearing someone being murder. All I could do was silently cry and hope the killer didn't find me.

## CHAPTER 27

They found the both of us lying under a pile of leaves and a log in the woods. Apparently, we weren't the only survivors. Two people made it out and were able to call the police. They both were badly injured. You don't know how happy I was when I saw my mother and father standing by the police cars.

I ran into their arms. It was the first time that I had let Shawn go. Hugging them made me cry even harder. The thought that Danielle wouldn't be able to do the same and the fact that it could've been me. There were going to be a lot of parents not bringing their kids home alive that day.

There was a light shining brightly in my eyes through the cracks of the log; indicating that the sun was starting to come up. I wasn't sure if this was a good sign or not. Who knows if the killer is still out there.

Shawn had managed to fall asleep somehow. I was too scared to go to sleep so I told him to get some rest while I kept a lookout. He was reluctant but happen to do so anyway. I knew he was pretty tired after what he was doing out there.

Shawn started to groan indicating that he was waking up. He shot up fast and let out a small cry. I covered his mouth to stop us from being heard. "Shh." His eyes widen. "Rayna." He grabbed me tight. I hugged him back knowing we both needed the comfort. "I thought I lost you." "Bad dream." "Yes, too bad it all wasn't a dream." I closed my eyes tight realizing what he meant. "I know." "Did you get any sleep?" "No, I couldn't I just couldn't." "Come on lay down. Everything is going to be okay. Someone will come for us. I just know it." "Do you think he is still out there?" "I'm not sure."

The atmosphere became quiet and the air seemed to grow thick. "Shawn I'm scared," I whispered. "You don't have to worry I'm not going to let anything happen to you alright. Do you understand?" I nodded my head. "Good, try to get some rest." I relaxed in his arms hoping to find some sort of comfort to ease my nerves.

"You never told me what you went back for. What happened what did you do?" "I just went back to see if anyone was still alive and try to find something to reach home, the police or something." "Was anybody still alive?" "I'm not sure." "Well, what about Kirk and." "Rayna." He said cutting me off. "I really don't know." "Shawn." "Shh." He hushed me. I became still as a rock because I heard it too. Something was out there.

Trying to be still and quiet as I can I closed my eyes and held my breath. It was attentional but more so fright. Shawn noticed my stillness and begin rubbing my back to calm me down. "It's okay." He whispered in my ear over. I felt a slight tickle in my ear sending a chill through my body.

I begin to pray silently hoping that we make it out of here alive. I started to pray that I would see my mommy and daddy again. I prayed that Danielle family will be okay with the news of their daughter. Most of all I prayed for the whole camp.

The crackling noise against the leaves was getting heavier. The sound appeared to be close to us. Grumbling and moaning escape the lips of whoever was out there. There was a loud thud on the ground. "Och." We heard someone say.

"Someones out there." Shawn laid me next to him as quietly as he can and started to get up. "Shawn no what are you doing." "Someone is out there and they sound like they are hurt." "I get that but what if." "Nothing will happen. I promise just stay here." He picked up some more leaves and spread them over my body. After he was done with that he lifted the log up just a bit to peak out.

Once I saw him remove the log completely I grab his arm."W hat are you doing?" I whispered to him. "Its okay just lay back down," He said. He pulled himself up and climbed out placing the log back over me. I sat up and peak from under the log. I don't care what he says I'm not letting anything happen to him either. I can't lose anyone else.

I watched as he slowly walked over to someone laying face down on the ground. He sat down next to the person and laid his head down placing his ear to the person's chest. He turned around facing me and frowned. "I thought I told you to stay down." He jumped when he realized the person grabbed his arm. "Shawn." I squeezed my eyes shut.

"I'm so glad that someone is alive." "Counselor Mikey?" "Yeah, kid." "Are you hurt?" "Yeah, but I'll be okay. What about you? Are you out here by yourself?" "Um uh, no La'Rayna is out here with me." He sat up some and groan. "Look I'm going to need you to go back and hide wherever it is you were hiding. I'm going to try and get us some help. I'll be back." "Consuler Mikey your hurt." "I'll be okay La'Rayna now you and Shawn just hide. I'll be back for the both of you."

Cousler Mikey is actually one of my favorite counselors. He always treated us fair. He was one of the few nice counselors that Camp Lakeview has. I'm glad that he's still alive. Counselor Mike was one of the few that were really nice. Also, he was always there to help. If anyone had a problem he didn't try and blame anyone like Coach Cutlip he tried to solve it. and whenever his mom sent treats for him he would share them with us. It was like he really cared about us.

"Why can't we just go with you." "Because I'm not sure whats out there. Besides, it will be faster if I just go alone. Less of us that will get spotted. Please just hide for now." "Okay." Shawn climbed back down into the hole that we were in and laid the log back over it. "Do you think hes going to find help." "I don't know he looked like he was hurt pretty bad." "What about you, are you okay?" "Yeah I'm fine."

I could tell that he was still in pain. He hurt himself pretty bad. I wasn't able to really doing anything about it. We found something to wrap it up but that was pretty much all that we could do. "You don't have to lie." "I'm not lying. Yeah, it hurts but I'm fine. I'll be okay. Get some rest and stop worrying. We can't stay here forever." "But Cousloer Mikey said." "I know what he said but we can't stay here. We can't count on him to come back." "I guess your right."

A few hours of rest and it was night almost night time again. Shawn was right we couldn't count on Counselor Mikey to get help. He was in pretty bad shape himself. If we wanted to make it out of this camp alive we had to find a way to help ourselves. I had awoken from my sleep an hour ago. I lay quite trying to let Shawn get some rest before we head off.

I felt Shawn shift beside me then he groaned out in pain. "Are you okay?" I whispered to him as he was waking up. "Um yeah I'm fine." "it getting dark outside do you still want to leave?" "Yeah, it would be for the best. That way it would be easier for us to hide. I don't know whats going on back at camp." We weren't necessary on campgrounds anymore but we were still a good distance by.

He was right the killer could very well still be out there doing who knows what. We also don't know who was still alive besides cosuler Mike of course. Or who might have been involved in the killings? I mean I just don't think that one man could do all of this to a whole camp.

"Before we leave we have to have some type of a plan." "Like what?" "If anything happens I want you to keep on running no matter what. Its no good if both of us end up dead." "Shawn." "No, listen to me okay. Just do as I saw." "Okay." "Okay, then when we get up to start moving I want you to take this and keep about 5 paces ahead." He said handing me the metal pipe we found back at camp. "I will control the back and you control the front." "We have to keep our eyes open and be sharp. We can take a break about every 30 minutes."

We removed the log that laid over the hole we were in and climbed above. I dust some of the leaves off of me while I wanted for Shawn to check the surrounding area. He pulled out a compass that he held in his pocket. "Well since we know that camp is that way we need to head this way. I remember there is a dirt road that led to the high way we came off to Camp Lakeview." "Well, do you know which direction it was in?" "No, but I do know that counsler Mike went in that direction for help. I figure if we head this was we can still move in the direction if where he was going but not be in clear distance of anything that he might have run into." "And places to hide." "Yeah."

We headed in the direction of Shawn compass. I did as he said and stayed a few paces ahead just in case anything happened. The sky was getting darker and it was becoming harder to see. We have been walking for about 30 minutes now and at this point, I was exhausted. We haven't eaten in two days and hardly slept for the fear of dying.

"Okay, we can take a break now." I felt Shawn closer to me making chills run down my spine. "Oh my gosh you scared me." "I'm sorry." "Its fine I just didn't know you were so close." "Here." He said handing me a water bottle. Thats the only thing we had.

He sat down slowly on a huge rock that was near a tree. He was injured badly I just didn't know how he got injured. When I went back I found him bleeding on the ground. I couldn't see the extent of his wound because it was so dark but I know he was hurt pretty bad. We ran to the nurse office and grabbed a bange and some rubbing alcohol to put on the wound.

"Shawn are you sure you are okay?" "Yeah, I'm fine my side just hurts a little thats all nothing too major." "Shawn." "Rayna I'm fine." "You told me that but it doesn't stop you from taking this water and drinking it." He smirked at me taking the drink. "Don't get smart." "Stop being so stubborn. Should we continue our walk?"

We continued on our little hike to the high way for another good two hours with little breaks in between. These woods felt like they kept going on and on. It was like we were never going to reach an end. I knew Shaw couldn't last any longer. I wanted to stop long ago but he wanted to push on. I didn't blame him.

I looked up at the sky and it seems to be about midnight. I knew Shawn could continue and I was pretty tired myself.

"Shawn I think we should break until dawn." "Are you sure because I can keep going." "Yes, we haven't eaten in days now. If we leave by dawn maybe we can find something to eat when daylight breaks. Besides I'm pretty exhausted." "Okay fine." I'm glad he didn't try to protest but I'm pretty sure he was just as exhausted if not more himself.

I sat down by a tree while Shawn tried to figure out a place for us to hide. He was pretty good at that so I wasn't going to stop him. My perfect hiding spot id being a bush. "Rayna, there's another ditch over there. I found a log but I need help moving it." I got up and saw the ditch that he was talking about. It looked as if he already covered parts of it with leaves to make it seem more natural. I helped him place the log over the ditch just enough to close the gap but for us to fit in a small space to crawl inside.

Before we crawled inside I offered to clean and change his bandage. I removed the old one and pour water on the wound to clean it up a bit. I took a piece of cloth and pour rubbing alcohol on it to wipe away any dirt and grim and wrapped it back up. I hid the dirty bandage in the dirt. We climbed down into the hole to rest.

I heard dogs barking. I tried to ignore it because I was so sleepy. Besides, where are dogs going to come from I must be dreaming? "Rayna wake up." I felt someone pushing me." "Rayna wake up I think someone is out there." "Uh, what are you talking about?' I slowly opened my eyes. "Do you hear that?" "Yeah, it sounds like dogs." I guess I wasn't dreaming.

"Hello is anybody out there. Any campers out there. We are not going to hurt you we are here to help." We heard different voices say. Our eyes widen in shock. We looked at each other reading each other's minds. The voices and barking got closer. I wasn't sure if we should move. Who knows what could be a tactic. Or perhaps counselor Mike found help. "Shawn." "Just what." He said knowing what I was going to say.

They found the both of us lying under a pile of leaves and a log in the woods. From the looks of it, we knew they weren't the killers. "We found some more survivors over here." A guy yelled. Another guy jumped down in the ditch. "Its okay we are here to help you. My name is Derek Morgan We are going to get you home okay." We didn't say anything we just nodded our heads. He lifted me up and another guy grabbed me out of the ditch. They did the same with Shawn.

"Are you two hurt." Again we didn't answer we just shook out heads. "Okay, we are going to get you guys some medical attention. They carried us a few feet away and there was a car there waiting for us. "Is there anyone else out there in the woods?" A woman asked us. We shrugged our shoulders. We didn't know anything and Shawn looked like he was going to pass out.

"Stay with us kid we are almost there." I noticed they were going back in the direction of camp. My eyes got wide and I made a screech sound. "Its okay other officers are there and your parents should be there as well. We are not going to hurt you." She was right because when we made it back to the camp there was a bunch of ambulance and police cars all outside. There was police tape all over the camp. And the blood. I had to look away. I leaned into Shawn and he wrapped his arms around me.

Everyone begin climbing out the car making me think we had to do the same. I really didn't want to set foot on this camp ever again. "We have to get you guys checked out." Mr. Morgan said. We both got out the car not letting each other go. They lead us over to the ambalance. I glanced around. Once I saw my parents I knew that I was safe. They were standing frantic talking to the police.

You don't know how happy I am when I saw my mother and father standing by the police cars. I ran into their arms. It was the first time that I had let Shawn go. Hugging them made me cry even harder. The thought that Danielle wouldn't be able to do the same and the fact that it could've been me. There are going to be a lot of parents not bringing their kids home alive today.

I was sitting in my room not wanting to come out. If I did I was afraid that something out there would get me. My mother and father came to my room to get me to talk, leave, anything. But I didn't budge. I was too traumatized by the events that took place last night.

Most of the camp was slaughtered. Shawn and a handful of others survived. I heard that Shawn is still in the hospital. He had a wound on his side that end up getting infected. They don't know if he's going to make it.

Here I lay with only a few cuts and bruises and Shawn maybe dying. I may be losing another friend. How could I come out of this room alive while everyone else around me is dead? It's just not fair. And Danielle its all my fault I should've stayed and helped. I should've done more.

There was a knock at my door but I didn't answer. I haven't spoken since yesterday when they found us and that was to Shawn. It wasn't that I was afraid to speak it was more so of what to say. What was I supposed to say? I guess this is what they mean when people become so traumatized they can't speak.

"Hey, sweetheart." My mother said as she walked into my room. I didn't respond. "Are you feeling better." Still, I said nothing. I could tell on her face that she knew that was a dumb question to ask. "Your father and I talked. We thought it would be a good idea if you went to go see someone. Like, talk to someone other than us about what happened. I know you aren't speaking right now but in a few weeks. Maybe you can open up to them. It's not going to be easy but Rayna you are going to have to talk about it sometimes. It's not good to keep stuff in. Especially something like that."

My dad walked in with a tray of food and set it down on the table in my room. "I made some of your favorites princess." I didn't move. I just wasn't in the mood for anything right now. All I really wanted to see was Shawn. I wanted to know if he was okay. He walked over to me and touched my shoulder. I jumped at the feeling. I don't know why but I did. The look on my fathers face would break anybody's heart. He brushed it off and spoke again. "Shawn is still in the hospital. I was thinking that maybe we could go tomorrow and see him."

I don't know if it was the look on my face but that seems to bring a little hope in my parent's eyes. Of course, I wanted to go see Shawn. I needed to know if he was going to be okay. He did everything that he could to protect me. He was hurt but not once let me know. He had to be okay.

"So, its settle we will go and see Shawn tomorrow at noon." "Eat up and get some rest." My mother said before they left out of the room. I just really hope that Shawn is okay but I'm glad that I get to go and see him.

# 28

## Chapter 28

I sat next to Shawn hospital bed while he slept. He's been sleeping since I first arrived. His wound was deeper than we both thought and he lost a lot of blood. And since it was clean or stitched up properly he ends up getting an infection. They thought he wouldn't make it if his infection spread to anywhere else in his body. They are keeping him here for a few nights to make sure that it doesn't happen.

All I had was a few cuts and bruises and a nasty gash on my left leg. It wasn't that bad so they leaned me up and I was able to leave with my parents. A police officer tried to talk to us but I was so shaken up that I didn't want to speak to anyone. There were two people that survived that was able to run and get help to send back to the camp.

So many people had lost their lives. They said it was one of the biggest massacres in history.

Back at camp when they were checking us out. Before we were sent off to the hospital. I saw Kirk sitting in a cop car rocking back and forth. His eyes were bucked and he looked as if he was chanting something. I don't know what happened to him after him and Shawn split up. I four sure that he was dead like everyone else.

Some of the parents have come together. I guess when an experience like this happens to your kids you have nothing else to do but support one another. I overheard my parents talking to Kirks about how they had to put him in a psych ward. All he was doing was yelling and screaming that he was right the whole time but nobody believed him. It had gotten to the point where he would just yell I knew it over and over.

His parents were telling mines this because my mom and dad were considering about putting me in one. That got me thinking. Are we insane? What happened to us out there did that make us crazy.

"Rayna." My head shot up so fast. "Shawn." He turned his head and looked at me. "Are you alright?" I nodded my head. "Good thats good." He looked around the room realizing where he was. "So, we made it uh." I nodded my head again. I don't know what it is but I just can't seem to speak. I shocked myself by saying his name but I think for now that's as far as its going to go.

"Do you know whats going on?" I shook my head no. "Its okay Rayna you can talk to me." I didn't say anything. I didn't know how to say anything. How can I when everyone is dead. I started to cry. Shawn sat up and pulled me into a hug. All I do is cry and I can't seem to stop.

Today is the day that I go and see a psychologist. We have to drive so far out that I don't even know where we are going. I'm sitting in the car watching a bunch of trees pass me by. I keep having flashes of camp. I close my eyes tight trying to get rid of these images.

"Hi Rayna, My name is Dr. Lambert." I didn't say anything. "I know what happened to you was very traumatic. Before we get into that do you want to discuss what it was like at camp before everything happened." I still didn't say anything I just kept looking at the floor.

"I know that this may be hard to discuss but I'm only here to help. Do you think it would be better if we talked about something else." I didn't want to talk I just want to get out of here. This guy. He didn't seem friendly at all and he reminded me of the killer. He looked down at his desk and picked up a silver piece of something. I didn't get a good look at it but I saw it shine in the light. It freaked me out like it was a knife or something. I got up and ran out.

I heard that Shawn is doing pretty good. I haven't seen him since he left the hospital. I don't really leave the room unless its to go see another psych.

I have terrible nightmares like I'm still at camp. I wake up every night screaming and crying. My dad comes in the room to calm me down but I freak out even more at his touch. I know I make him sad. He comes into my room at night in the middle of my freak session. Since all I see is a shadow figure I get scared all over again. So, I try not to go to sleep anymore. I don't think that I can take seeing those same images reply continuity.

I sit in the corner of my room looking at a picture of Danielle and I. Tears falling down my face. I'm so sick of crying but I don't know what else to do. It hurts so much. We went to her funeral the other day. I could tell that her parents hate me.

I walked up to her casket to take one last look at her before the closed it. I placed her half of a best friend necklace in there. When I turned around her mother was looking at me with so much disgust. I understand. I hate myself. I hate myself for pushing her to go with me, I hate my self for not helping her, I hate myself for not going back.

It should be me lying there in that casket and not her. My foot is the one that got stuck. I should've told her to go on without me. I should've never called her back. And now she is dead because of me. She's dead and all I did was watch.

**29**

## CHAPTER 29

The candlelight service was tonight. With the help of the camp director that Shawn hired I was able to pull it off. She was a big help. We invited the family of the ones who died and the local people in the neighboring town. She even got the news crew to come out to cover the story.

We decided to have the candlelight service just outside of the campgrounds. We didn't want to have it inside the camp because Shawns wants to have the big reveal tomorrow when the camp opens. He didn't want anybody to know how much the camp has changed, look wise until the day of the opening. The only people who know how the camp looks are the staff and the contractors of course.

I was sitting in Shawn's office while he was away at the mess hall having a meeting with his staff. Tomorrow was the big day so they had a few last minute things to talk about. As for me, I was putting together the rest of the flower arrangements and candles.

The candlelight service

The sun was setting giving off a beautiful light to the sky. The candlelight service was just about to start. Candles were being passed out to everyone who came. There were yellow flowers spread around the area representing love and friendship. there was a banner that held everyone's name who had lost their lives that night. At the last minute, Marin the camp director was able to get a blown up picture of the one we took years ago at camp. The site was really beautiful to say and I'm sure everyone who died would love this. I'm glad we are honoring and cherishing their life.

A speech by Shawn

"Opening Camp Lakeview back up wasn't an easy task for me to complete. As many of you know what took place here 15 years ago. 15 years ago there was a mass murder and unforatanlly had to live through that.

Although I am glad that I survived there are others that have lost their lives. People may look back at what happened as a tragedy in which it was but I'm sure that those who passed on would want us to cherish and honor their life.

I wasn't too thrilled when I found out that my father bought this place and decided to reopen it. In fact, I was against it and tried everything that I could to stop it. I had to come to the realizing of letting go and moving on. Its what I know my friends who have left me would want.

We open up Camp Lakeview in memory of those we love that passed on. This camp is for them. This camp is a symbol of hope and new beginnings."

On the back of the picture, Marin thought it would be a great idea to write something to the person we list that night. Overall the service turned out pretty nice. I just know that everyone who died that night would love this. And everyone who lost someone that night was able to get a little bit of closure.

Standing there looking at Danielle parents was surreal. I haven't seen them since the day they found us. The hurt look on their faces as they watched their daughters best friend re-unite with their parents. The frantic look on their faces searching for their daughter and me realizing that Danielle wasn't about to walk out of that camp alive.

I'm not really sure what happened to our relationship. Danielle parents were my godparents. But after the incident, I never spoke to them ever again. Sometimes I feel like they blamed me for their daughter's death. At times I do too.

Shawn was over there carrying on a conversation with Danielle parents. It's like the never missed a beat. I slowly walked over there. Part of me wanted to be noisy and the other part just really wanted them to forgive me.

"Shawn its really nice seeing you again." "Yes, I'm glad that we can still connect after all these years." "And as I can see from here the camp looks so lovely and this ceremony was so nice. Danielle would've loved it." "Well, I would like to take credit for this but La'Rayna is the one that set this whole thing up. All of this was her idea." Shawn pulled me next to him. Danielle parents eyes shifted towards me for a split second. "Hi, Mr. and Mrs. Jonhson" They didn't respond. Mrs. cleared his throat and spoke to Shawn. "Well, we will see you later Shawn." "Yeah every third Wednesday of each month, Now don't you forget." "Have I ever." They gave him a hug and walked away.

That really just hurt me more than anything. Like I wasn't there and my feeling didn't even matter. I wanted to break down and cry right there. I pulled away from Shawn. "Rayna." "No, no you have been in contact this whole time with them." "Yeah but." "And you never told me," I said cutting him off. "This whole time huh. All those times I vent to you about how they seem like they hated me and was shutting me out for what happened and you were still in contact with them. My best friends parents, my supposed godparents." "La'Rayna I'm sorry I didn't tell you because I knew it would upset you." "Well, it's nice to know that I still have a friend." "La'Rayna come on."

He grabbed my arm but I pulled away. I just wanted to be alone. I found myself wandering around the camp. I ended up in front of my old cabin. Cabin five now known as the sunflower cabin. It was so bright here. For some reason, things still looked the same. No matter how much paint and decoration you put up it just can't hide the pain that happened here.

I walked over to the back where we tried to escape. Flashes of blood being splattered on the wall. Screams echoing in my ear.

Rayna and Danielle being screamed. The creepy camp song being sung followed by giggling. Never go over the hill...soon your soul will end...the cabin is at a dead end...cabin six that is...searching through the wasteland that is...they never found his body...now he's hunting everybody...you'll be next...he's coming for you with an ax...living at Camp Lakeview...gotta sleep with one eye open...or he's gonna get you."

I heard the door slammed shut making me jump and fall out of the trace that I seemed to be in. I turned around and there stood Kirk in the doorway. What could he be doing here? I didn't even notice him in the crowd of people during the ceremony.

"Whoa, this place looks a bit different. Don't you think Ray Ray?" "Please don't call me that." "Oh, haven't we become the polite one." He walked closer to me. "What are you doing here?" "I came to warn you." "Warn me. Warn me about what?" "Shawn didn't tell you." "Tell me what? Get to the point." "Something isn't right. Something isn't right here. You shouldn't open this camp." "Then why are you sending your niece here then huh." "I'm not sending her nowhere. I have no control over what my sister does. Besides I tried to warn her too. But that's why I'm coming to you."

# 30

## CHAPTER 30

Today is the first day of camp. Camp Lakeview will be opening its doors in over 15 years. Shawn has been running across the camp making sure that everything runs smooth. I can understand his nervousness. I was there with him 15 years ago. I heard the talk around town after everything happen. The plans to reopen the camp took a lot of convincing from his father.

Trying to access the blueprints, the buying of the land and to greenlight its relaunch to the public wasn't a joke. A lot of people had their doubts and dared not to send their kids here. The ones who survived grew up. It's our kids that would be coming here. However, I don't blame them. This camp stole our innocence from us.

I was standing in the back watching Shawn give a speech to the new camp counselors. Sort of a pep talk before the kids arrive on the buses. To say that I was proud of him would be an understatement. The strength that he shows is unbelievable. I'm just glad I was here to witness it.

Shawns little speech

"We chose this group of people to work here because we believe in your ability to work with children. We are trying to change what went on here years ago and spread love, light, and positivity in the daily lives of these kids. A lot of these kids don't have a lot of things to look forward to. Their hope is in this camp. They are here to have a great time and forget about the things that they have going on back home. This camp will be their safe haven."

"I know some of you have heard of the rumors that went on at this camp 15 years ago. Some of you were just babies or may not have been born yet. I'm here to tell you that those are not rumors because I lived through those moments. I don't want these kids to live the same thing that I did."

"We have been training you guys for months now and I see that you all have what it takes to make sure that the dreams of these kids will not die. If you guys have any questions or concerns please do not hesitate to ask. My office is always open and you can speak to the camp director when I'm not around. I don't want this place to just be a fun place for the kids but to you as well. I want this to be a fun place for you to work at. I want you to be able to get up and be ready to work. But I want you to be happy to be ready to work. I want to thank everyone who has made this possible and lets open up this camp."

Everyone begins to clap after Shawn was done speaking. The Camp Director and Assisting director let all the counselors know where to set up and to pick up their schedules and group activity handouts and what not.

"So how did I do?" "It was great. Your father would be proud." "I sure hope so. I don't want to let him down. This is the first project that he let me have complete control over you know.

We were all on our way to greet the kids and the families as they were coming off the bus. "Are you nervous?" "Very, it took a lot to convince people to consider letting their kids come to this camp." "I bet." "I mean if I'm able to come back here what is it to stop someone else. I lived through it. We lived through it and look at us." "Shawn I'm sure there are kids on the bus. Everything is going to be fine."

I understood where Shawn was coming from more than anybody obviously. Rebuilding this camp had to be hard on him. The things we both went through here... But Shawn has always been strong. He knows how to put his feelings aside for other people. No matter what he is going through he would drop it all for someone else. It's like others pain are even greater than his.

We watched the busses and cars pull onto the road leading down to the camp. "Well, this is it." "No, turning back," Shawn said.

"I would like to thank each and every one of you for coming here today. I know what may happen here years ago was a tragedy. But it was that years ago. I can assure you that this camp is different. That this time it will be different. I don't want another family to go through the same thing as mines did. But we are here to celebrate the new opening of Camp Lakeview. I welcome you and hope that you have a great summer."

Shawn grabbed the giant scissors from one of the staff and cut the red ribbon that was tied to each poll entrance of the camp while everyone begins to clap. Camp Lakeview is officially open.

"Hello, and welcome my name is Marie and I am the Camp Director. These are our wonderful staff. We will be splitting the kids up by school grade and colors. Each group will be assigned a counselor and a cabin name. We will go over some rules and question and be following a tour. Marie went on to explain to the parents and campers things that will be going on in camp. "You all may follow me into the mess hall."

I went over and leaned on Shawn's shoulder watching the kids and their parents follow everyone into the camp for the first time in 15 years. "You did it." "Yeah, we did." "Are you staying here to see how the camp is run or?" "I plan on staying here for a few weeks to oversee everything." "Well, I guess I'm staying too."

A few weeks have gone by since the first day of camp. Things seem to be running smoothly. The camp started off great and the kids love it. Shawn has already received a ton of praise from the community and the parents back home for how the camp has been going.

The news crew came back out here to film the progression of the camp so far and Camp Lakeview was even in the paper. It was voted online the number one camp of the summer. On top of that people have already started signing their kids up for camp next year.

Since the camp has received such great news Shawn's father looked into his idea of having the camp open for a week in the winter. Shawn was so excited that he came up with plans to do already.

Camp Lakeview is nothing like it was when we were here. The kids have access to lots more activities, such as archery, boating, pottery, zip lining, water skiing, and even real hiking trips. We weren't allowed to go off into the woods. It was forbidden. Few of our activities required us to go into the woods but we were never supposed to leave the trail. As you can see why?

Letters are still being sent home. Shawn wanted to teach kids how to write letters and the feeling of writing something personal to someone they love. Since the kids are not allowed to have electronics out here for the fear of being lost or stolen they can call home using the office phone. He was making sure we are not shut off from the outside world. If anything happens we are able to reach someone.

The main thing is cabin six. It still spooks me out and having all the kids run in and out doesn't help either. That place was forbidden when I was a kid now its an open door. I understand that its now the camps official store but the outside doesn't help. Kids already made up some scary stories about the place.

"Legend has it a long time ago when the camp was fairly new." Gerald deemed by the kids at camp the keeper of the tales started telling the story to a group of kids. I just had to shake my head and laugh. These kids were something else. They reminded me a lot of us when we were here.

Walking around this place I sometimes still get flashes of what went on here years ago. Right now I was helping the kids out in the craft room. "Ms. Rayna can you help me mix my slime. It's not turning out like yours." "Yes, sure let's see what happened." Each week the camp has a theme. This weeks theme is science camp so right now we are having the kids make slime.

"Ah, I see you put too much liquid in here making it watery. All we have to do is add more of this to thicken it back up." "Woah cool thanks, Ms. Rayna." "No problem. Does anybody else need any help with their slime?"

Being here with these kids gave me something back that was stolen a long time ago. A sense of security and just good old fun. I was actually really enjoying myself. Something that I haven't been able to do in a long time. Being here made me think back on the old times that we had at camp. Although for us things turned out horrible we did have fun back then.

No matter what I will never get over how I feel. The camp may look a bit different and the environment may have lifted but I still will never forget. I lived through one of the worst things possible. Those days I could never forget no matter how hard I tried. Especially after what Kirk told me. My mind still goes back to that day.

"Whoa, this place looks a bit different. Don't you think Ray Ray?" "Please don't call me that." "Oh, haven't we become the polite one." He walked closer to me. "What are you doing here?" "I came to warn you." "Warn me. Warn me about what?" "Shawn didn't tell you." "Tell me what? Get to the point." "Something isn't right. Something isn't right here. You shouldn't open this camp." "Then why are you sending your niece here then huh." "I'm not sending her nowhere. I have no control over what my sister does. Besides I tried to warn her too. But that's why I'm coming to you."

I squinted my eyes at him as he moved closer. I'm not too sure that I could trust him. He was put into a facility. He couldn't be all the way there. "I'm coming to you because I know that you are the only one who will listen." He said. "Listen to what?" "To what I have to say. Shawn did want to hear it. I know since you were the one back then." "The one." "Yes, you are the one. You were the one that all the clues went to. You are the chosen one. The chosen one."

I just knew that he was crazy. His mind was gone. What happened back then sure did damage to him. I mean sure I was the one who had a feeling that something was going on. Part of that was because I was a scary cat. "We all had that feeling thats why we went looking for what we went looking for." "No, you are the one!" He yelled at me maing me jump.

To be honest I was scared of him. He had this crazy look in his eyes. And the way he was dressed. It was for a show or something. It was like he was dressed for a business meeting but that he had the clostes for years. I guess he could sense my uneasiness. "I'm sorry. I didn't mean to yell. You just have to know the truth."

"Kirk what is going on." "Promise me." "Promise you what." "Promise that you will believe me." "Tell me whats going on?" "Ylou just have to promise me. Promise me those kids wont get hurt. Don't let them end up like us."

He started going off on a rant. I tried to think of a way to get out of here and away from him. "They locked me up because they wanted to shut me up. The called me crazy. I'm not crazy. I know the truth. And so do you. We all do. And to think that Shawn would open this camp up. I tried to warn him Ray Ray. I did. You have to listen to me."

"Just tell me already!" I yelled at him. "The killer is still alive. He's back." After he said those words my heart skipped a beat. "They covered it up they tried to cover it up." "But why?" I whispered. "Why would they?" He started to say something else but Shawn walked through the door.

"Is everything okay? I heard yelling." He said looking between Kirk and me. "It was nothing he just startled me." I didn't like lying to Shawn but He was keeping secrets from me as well. I'll tell him when the time is right. I just hope he will do the same.

# 31

## CHAPTER 31

Its been a few months now since the camp has been open. Its almost the end of summer which means the end of the camp will be coming soon. Shawn and I decided to head back down to Camp Lakeview to check on the progress. Even though he knew it was doing well he just wanted to be sure.

I was in my room packing a few things for the trip back. I still can't believe that I was going back to Camp Lakeview for the second time this year in 15 years. I wouldn't say that I have gotten over everything that has happened nor am I any better mentally. I still go see my therapist. I even started talking to her now. I haven't opened up to her about what happened in the past or how I'm feeling about it. We kind of just talked.

"Come in," I said to whoever was knocking at my door. "Rayna." I heard my mother say as I continue to pack. "La'Rayna stop packing I want to talk to you." "Talk about what?" "About your progress about everything that has been going on." "I'm not some experiment mom." "I know that. I just want us to talk. I care and worry about you. You know. Ever since what happened we haven't talked. You talk to Shawn. And you are doing so well now that I just want to talk."

I stopped speaking to everyone after what happened to us at Camp Lakeview. I barely spoke to Shwan when we came back. Those that survived were locked up in mental institutions. Those of us who came from money like Shawn and I had parents that refused to let us be thrown into those circumstances.

I was so happy to be home and to see my parents again. At the same time, I felt like I should've died because I wasn't able to save Danielle. What I went through back there at Camp Lakeview no kids should have to experience. I was depressed and traumatized. I would freak out over the little things. I hated being in small spaces and I was terrified of blood. I could no longer listen to music or watch TV. Every day I lived in the memory of camp with sleep terrors. Not only was I seeing flashes throughout the day but I would dream about it at night.

On top of all that I watched my family fall apart. My mother and father argued every day about how crazy I was and that I need to get some real help. My father wanted to ship me off somewhere but my mother wasn't haven't it. She didn't want anyone to label me as a crazy person. In the end, my mother lost the fight because my father walked out on us and I never saw him again.

He would call every now and then just to check up on me but since I never talked to anyone not even on the phone he gave up. He started to write to me and send money but that wasn't enough. I never wrote back. If he really cared he would've never left. He still writes to me but I stopped reading the letters.

I end up being kind of jealous of Shawn. He was way stronger then I could ever be. He was able to move on. He finished school on time, went on to college, and started a career. His parents never split up. It was like his family cared more for him to actually stay and help him.

"Mom, I'm doing fine." "I know and I see that. I'm proud of you. Your father is too." I didn't respond to that. I didn't know how. "Everything that has happened." "Mom, I don't want to talk about that." "When will you be ready?" "Well, let me check to see what the time limit is on a child who watched an entire camp get slaught while almost losing their lives in the process." "Rayna." "No, that was the problem that was always the problem you guys were always pushing it. You guys tried to get me to pretend it never happened but it did. Then dad called me crazy."

Her face saddening. "You heard that." "I heard everything." "I never meant for you to hear those conversations." "It doesn't matter if you meant to I still heard them and it still affected me." "I'm sorry." "I wish you guys would've done more than I'm sorry." "Rayna," she called my name.

I looked in the doorway and saw Shawn standing there. He cleared his throat. "I'm sorry but um we should get going. I don't want to be on the road at night." "Um yes, you guys should get going. I packed some food for you guys to take with you." "You didn't have to do that Mrs. B." Shawn picked up my bag and headed towards the door. My mother gave me and hug and whispered something in my ear. "Be safe."

Back at Camp

We have been back at camp for a few days now. Things seemed to be running smoothly from what the camp director told. She's one of those fake it to you make it type people. Al the consolers apparently hate her. Shes nice and all she just doesn't know what shes doing. Lets just say she doesn't know how to lead a team.

At least the kids seem to be enjoying themselves. I think thats all that really matters at this point. I was helping Shawn inspect some of the cabins making sure everything was in order. One of the counselor's names Kelsey was in there with me. She was talking my ear off.

"She is kind of pain you know.She's a nice old lady. She doesn't really have ay real people skills. And she doesn't deal with the kids in a respectful way. Their kids I mean they don't handle stuff like you and me." "Is that right." "Yeah, so do you know if Shawn is looking for a replacement?" I just looked at her.

"So, everything seems to be working fine in here correct?" I asked changing the subject. "Yes, I haven't had any problems." "And the kids. They are doing okay?" "Yes, they are fine. Um but there is this one girl. She doesn't get along with anybody. She likes to pick on the other girls. We talked to her several times." "What's her name?" "She likes to go by Mel. Something about her being named after her mom's cousin. I don't know?" "Try calling home to see if they can give you any insight."

Before she rambled on Shawn came into the cabin. "Rayna." "Yes." "I'm going to need you to come with me." "What's going on?" "I'll get to that later. Kelsey I'm going to need you to meet up with your co coulsner for this cabin and gather all the kids from this cabin." "And then what?" "JUst make sure yolu have everyone. Wait for futher instructions."

We walked out of the cabin and headed towards his offcie. "Whats going on?" He didn't answer me until we were further away from people. "Someone is missing." That moment I had strange flashes of deja vu.

"So what's the plan. Are you going to send everyone home?"I said as we walked into his office.  "That's the thing." "What?" "I can't." "What do you mean you can't send everyone home? Shawn someone went missing." "I get that but that doesn't change the fact. I can't send everyone home I don't have the means and sources. to do so." "What what are we supposed to do wait until more kids go missing. I will not let what happened years ago happen again."

Shawn looked at me with so much anger. "And you think I would? Huh is that what you think of me." He yelled. I had nothing to say. "There you go being selfish again and not thinking of others feelings." "I'm sorry." "That's right you are."

At that moment my feelings were hurt. I just wanted to get away from this camp. "Rayna wait. I'm sorry I didn't mean it. I hear what you are saying but I just can't do it. But I promise that I will not let anything happen to those kids. I put that on my life. Besides I already had Marie contact all the parent to let them know what was going on. We took all the necessary steps in case something happened like it did years ago. I would've never opened up this camp if we didn't look out for the best interest of these kids."

"Besides I don't want to jump to conclusions. He may have just gotten lost. They were out hiking with Kevin. A kid that was on the hike told me that he saw him just before they made it back to camp. Maybe he stopped or saw something that leads him away from the others. Kevin told me when they go back is when he counted all the kids one last time and that's when he realized he was missing."

Shawn sat down and went over the plans with me and everything that went down with Lucus the missing camper. They planned everything out to ensure everyone's safety. It made me feel bad for jumping to conclusions. There is so reason nor evidence to think that the same killer is out there to come back after all these years to kill again.

Apparently, Lucus and a group of them went exploring in the woods for nature camp this week. The idea was to see what you can find out in the woods to learn survival skills for camping or if something happened. Somehow Lucus got separated from everyone else and no one has seen him since.

To ensure that the other campers wouldn't freak out they tried to spread the fact that everything will be okay and that they are doing everything to find him. His group said that his pack of supplies was with him. Shawn had a rescue team already in place in case of something like this. They are out there right now looking for him.

They put together emergency packs and everything for these kids. If there is one little sign that something more is going on he will have a team of buses come to pick up these kids to send them to a safe location. Right now the kids are not allowed anywhere near the woods and are not to cross over the lakeside.

Also, let all the parents know what is going on and if they want to come to get their kids please do so as soon as possible to ensure they leave safe. But for now its nothing too serious like a death. He is just missing right.

"I'm not sure what could have gone wrong. I made sure everything was checked out. Every inch of this camp was inspected to ensure nothing like this would happen again." Shawn stated. "I'm pretty sure he's just lost those woods are huge." "I sent parties out there to look for him." "You don't really think." "I don't know man. Maybe he was right." "Maybe who was right."

There was only one person I knew he could be speaking of and that was Kirk. He was the only one that came here to warn us. I really just thought that he was bat crazy. Nothing he said made any sense. After all these years. I just don't know if I could believe. I have to know what Kirk told him. and what was in the letter.

"Shawn what did Kirk say. What did he want?" "What do you mean?" "When he came here months ago what did he say to you? What was in the envelope?" "How did you know about that?" "It doesn't matter I need to know what he said." "Nothing really. He just said some crazy stuff. You know he was locked up." "That's exactly why he why he came to me. He knew no one would believe him." "He came to you when what did he say to you?"

His face becomes hard then his eyes widen like he was putting two and two together. "When I caught you together in the sunflower cabin. Why would you lie to me?" "Well, you lied to me." "I told you he didn't want anything nor did he say anything." "Shawn he told me that the killer was still out there. That the police lied." "Come on Rayna why would that make sense. What do they have to lie for? How would he still be alive after all this time? Think about it Kirk is crazy."

"You're right I'm not going to deny that but. I don't know." "Don't give me that I don't know stuff we aren't going out there investigating. That almost got us killed last time. Besides I made sure everything was checked out. I would never want to open this place if I knew that." "I know but what if he left when we left. I never said anything because I always thought that I was crazy myself." "Rayna your not crazy." "Just listen to me. I always had this feeling like someone was watching me."

## 32

### CHAPTER 32

"You have to be kidding me." "Look I know it sounds crazy and you don't have to believe me." "Rayna I really don't want to hear this right now. We have a kid missing." "Yeah, and you didn't want to hear it back then either but I was right" "This isn't the same thing." "How come its not?" "Because he's dead okay. We made sure of it." "Did we?" "Why do you think I went back?"

All these years I never knew why Shawn went back. I remember begging him not to but I never asked him for his reasoning to go. When he came back he seemed like a different person and I didn't know why. I never questioned him. I never had to because I always trusted him. What other reason would he have to go back if it wasn't told bring anyone along? He never came back with anyone or anything.

"What happened?" He started to speak but was cut off by the door opening. "Mr. Weiss I'm sorry to interrupt. One of the counselors said shifting their eyes between Shawn and I. "But um there is some good news and um bad news." "Its okay come on in. So, what's going on." "Well, sir we found Lucus. But we um we found something else as well."

Hearing the words we found Lucus gave me relief. Maybe we were just jumping to conclusions but who could blame us. We have good reasons to.

"What's going on?" "You see we found Lucus hiding out in a cave. But he was covered in dry blood." "Oh my gosh is he okay?" "He may be a little shaken up but the blood wasn't his." "What do you mean the blood wasn't his?" "That's just it the blood wasn't his. Just before we found him in the cave we found a body out in the woods. At first, we thought it was him but the body seemed to be there for a while."

"How is that possible if Lucus end up with dry blood on him?" "I agree this isn't adding up." "Excuse me um we think that the little boy was killed recently." "Little boy?" "Yes, that's why we thought the little boy was Lucus at first." "Who could this little boy be everyone at camp has been counted for."

The bus company was only able to allow one bus to come to pick up the kids. They claimed it was because every other camp this summer already rented the buses as well and they are not responsible for Camp Lakeview itself. Shawn was furious. He was yelling on the phone demanding to send more to get these kids off the camp as soon as possible.

He put his head down shaking it. "What happened what did they say?" "That there was nothing they could do. That this was the only bus they had left to send. I mean we had a contract.

How am I supposed to get these kids off this camp." "Sir I'm guessing we have to send who we can. Its better than nothing." "He's right Shawn. As much as I hate saying this we have to send who we can." "How can I do that knowing what I know."

We gathered all the kids in Mckinly hall. We tried to explain the situation the best we could. We didn't want to scare the kids, especially the little kids. The other kids were fully aware of what was at stake. You can see in the eyes of a few who are choosing to stay behind and set the younger siblings ahead.

Shawn quited the room down so that he could address the situation at hand. Everyone didn't know what was going on and he wanted to keep it that way. He didn't want to scare anyone into a panic.

"I know you are all bummed that camp is ending sooner than expected. But I would rather keep everyone safe. Don't worry nobody is in danger. As you can see that Lucus was found and that he is okay. Everyone safety is the most important. We have to shut down in order to secure the camp. As of right now, the camp is on lockdown until transportation arrives. As soon as transportation arrives you will be lead out by your assigned coulser. Those of you who will be staying will receive further instructions."

We were outside with the kids getting them all ready to get on the bus to leave. "Its okay most of us are getting on the bus. A few of us just have to stay behind. I'm sure they are sending another bus. You will see me soon." I heard a kid tell their younger brother who was crying. "But why do you have to stay." "So you and your little friends can get on. Come on look at me a big tough guy like me isn't afraid of anything. I can handle it alright."

I just really hope things aren't turning out as they did years ago and that we are just being paranoid. I know that kid is being brave for his little brother. I promise that no harm will come to these kids.

"Rayna you don't have to stay." "What are you talking about." "I want you on that bus. I wouldn't want to put you through that again." "Shawn I can't leave. I can't leave you or these other kids here. Knowing what I know and that I selfishly got on that bus and took a spot from one of these kids."

We managed to get most of the kids on the bus. Although there were still a good amount of kids left behind. Only a few adults were allowed to go with the kids. In case something really was going on we split everyone up. We couldn't have everyone in one area to be slaughtered.

I was with Shawn and some of the kids. Shawn had set up certain areas of the camp that no one really knew about to hide. After the power source from the camp was shut off we knew something extremely wrong could happen. He calmed everyone down and issued out safety packs to the few counselors that stayed behind.

With the power being out and the fact that there was a thunderstorm going on outside it wasn't a surprise that people started to panic. Also, it didn't help that Derek never came back from cabin six. A couple of kids told us that when they were in the shop that they heard strange noises coming from the woods just beyond the cabin. Shawn was going to go and check it out but Dereck insisted that he should be the one to go instead. He had a background in hunting which led into him being hired Camp Lakeview in the first place.

Of course, as always Shawn tried to fight his way to going but Derek wouldn't accept. All the counselors and staff here know what went on years ago and they know that Shawn and I were two of the survives. It was obvious why Derek volunteer to go in the first place. Nobody wanted us to go through that again.

Shawn and I were standing off by a far corner talking but still making sure we were able to see the kids. "Shawn, what are we going to do?" "Relax everything is going to be fine. I won't let anything happen to you or these kids." "I just can't believe this is happening again." "Come on we don't know that." "What about the kid and the power being cut off." "The power cut off because of the storm outside. And the kid I'm not sure where he even came from. The police assured us that he was dead.

I knew Shawn was just trying to keep me calm. I had to be for these kids. If they suspect that anything is wrong with me it would be hard to control them. It will be hard to protect them. "Do you think we are going to get out of here?" "I'm going to make sure we do. I'm not letting what happened years ago happen again."

The nightmare all over again. I cannot believe this is happening again. Never in a million years would I think that I would ever be stepping foot back on these campgrounds again. And here I am again at Camp Lakeview scared for my life. Talk about history repeating itself. I know one thing for certain I will not let history take the innocent from these kids lie it did mines. I will protect them with everything I have in me.

We heard a strange noise just outside of the door. My heart started beating faster. It was almost like it was about to explode. The sound sounded all too familiar. I looked over at Shawn. I could tell by the look on his face that he knew what I knew.

"Shawn, what going on?" "I'm not sure but I know we can't stay here any longer." "What are you saying?" "Rayna listen to me. I want you to take the kids and get out of here." "What about you?" "We have to split up." I started to panic on the inside. There was no way that I was splitting up. Splitting up is how people get killed.

"No, no I'm not doing that I can't do that." "Listen to me, Rayna." "No, Shawn I can leave you. Splitting up gets people killed. You know what happened to Derker. And how am I supposed to get away with all these kids by myself." "We don't have a choice. Look I'll take some of the older kids and you take the younger ones. If anything happens I know that I can count on them to run as far away while I distract whoever is doing this. If you take the younger kids you guys will be able to hide out somewhere. To be honest you were always much better with kids than me." "Shawn I can't." "Yes, you can. I saw how you were early with them. They will feel safe with you. You have to trust me."

I trust Shawn with my life I just wasn't willing to let him risk his life for me. Not again. I heard what he said. Distracting the killer in order for us to get away. I didn't want him to do that. But the thing is he's right. It's better for us to split up and get out of here. It worked for us last time.

"I could easily take the younger ones and get out of here and hide. Him taking the older kids made more sense. They will be able to keep up the same pace as him if not more. and If something goes down nobody will have to worry about someone slowing us down. And we all couldn't stay together anymore. It's just not safe or practical. There's too many of us in one room. And if we want to get out of the camp alive we have to move and move fast."

I was willing to do whatever it takes. It was my turn to protect those close to me. Besides, there was no turning back now. "So what's the plan?"

Shawn and Rayna weren't the only ones that thought it was a good idea to get out of camp while they could. Shawns hideaway plans were only convenient for a short period of time. It was to trick the killer into thinking that they got everyone off camp grounds. Having a bunch of them in one area just wasn't a good idea nor was staying in camp.

Counselor Kelsey was the first to try and get her group of kids from the campgrounds.  Being that she was the closest to the front of the camp means that she should've had ample time to get the kids to safety.

"Counselor Kelsey." One of the little girls she had with her spoke up. "Yes, sweetheart." "Are we going home." "I'm going to try to get us home but first we must leave this camp." "What's going on?" "I'm not sure but its just not okay for us to be on campgrounds right now." She didn't want to alarm any of the kids by telling them that something was wrong. She chose her words very carefully, especially around the smaller children.

"What was that?" "I'm not sure. I bet its just someone trying to leave like us. Don't worry about."Kelsey was doing her best not to alarm the kids. That is until the heard the noise again. "I'm scared." "There's nothing to be scared of. We are going to be okay." No matter what she said to them the noise continues.

Soon Kelsey realized that sacrifice would be her best bet if she wanted to get these kids out alive. Pulling the oldest aside she knew what had to be done. "Alec I need you to take the kids and run. No matter what don't wait for me." "What do you mean?" A loud scream could be heard far off. "That, that is what I mean." "Miss Kelsey what's going on?" "I'm not quite sure. Just take the kids and go."

She shoved them towards the others and watched them take off in the distance. "Maybe I can throw them off track." She whispered. She didn't know what was out there but she was willing to face it. Little did she know someone wasn't far behind.

Kelsey thought it would be a great idea to take another journey through the woods. Her best bet was whoever was out there would follow her instead and leave the kids alone. She heard more screaming. "What is going on?" This time the screams were closer. "Help someone please help."

She headed towards the cries for help until someone pull on her arm. She screamed but they covered her mouth. "Shh before you get us caught." "Well I'm sorry but something strange is going on here and you pulling on me in the middle of these dark woods doesn't help that." "I'm sorry." "Wait Alec I thought I told you to go with the others." "I know but I sent them ahead."

She was furious. How is she supposed to save anybody if they don't listen? "Stay here I'm going to see who that is." "I'm not letting you go by yourself." She knew he wasn't going to listen so there was no use in arguing.

When the reached where the noise was coming from the didn't expect to see what they saw. "What is going on?" "Help me please." She rushed over to help the little girl on the ground. Meanwhile, Alec was in shocked at the sight that he saw before him. There were blood and bodies. It was like he was looking at a scene from a horror movie.

As Kelsey was helping the little girl off the ground a figure appeared before them. As they both looked up his arm was raised ready to slash them. Just as her eyes met his her fate was sealed. Alec wanted to move but he couldn't. As her head rolled over to his feet he peeped his pants. He knew he was next.

## 33

· · ·

## EPILOGUE

There was no way that we could stay in that building. We wouldn't be safe. The best way was for her to get out as fast as we could. Shawn thought it would be better for us to split up so we wouldn't track a lot of attention or be slowed down as a group. I try to talk him out of it but in the end, he won.

Splitting up is a sure fire way to be killed. Come on Rayna you can't think like this you have people counting on you. You can get through this you have before. I took a deep breath to calm my nerves. "Ms. Rayna are you okay?" "Yeah, I am fine. Thank you love." "Do you know what's going on?" "Yeah are we going home. I promise you that."

I didn't want to lie to them but I didn't want to tell them the truth. However, I'm not too sure what is really going on. "I don't want you guys to worry. Everything is going to be fine. I will make sure to keep you all safe while we are out here. I promise that you guys will make it home. I put that on my life." "But what happened?" "The power went out during the storm." "Why did we have to split up?" "Yeah, and why couldn't we all get on the bus?"

These kids were young so I know they didn't fully understand what Shawn had explained at the meeting in Mckinly hall. When we decided to leave the cabin that we were in Shawn made the decision for me to take the smaller kids. He suggested that I would be able to handle them in a more gentle and compassionate manner then he could. And being that there wasn't that many of them I agreed. Sure they were small and didn't really understand what was going on but they couldn't possibly slow me down as they would him.

"Well, something happened and they thought it was best to try and get as many people out of camp as they could. We all stayed behind because there just wasn't any room on the bus. We split up because it will be safer to travel in smaller groups." "So, where are we going?" "I'm going to try and get us out of here." "Are we going home?" "Not yet but we are going to a safe place."

I planned on taking them to the spot where Shawn and I went when this happened to us 15 years ago. It was the only place I knew they could fit and be safe. Once I leave them there I will go back for Shawn. The rain was really helping. It was harder to cover our tracks because of the mud but it was also hard to see us.

We heard screams far off into the distance. Those type of screams were all too familiar. "What was that?" I don't know and I don't want to find out. "Come on let's keep going."

The sky was getting darker and the air was getting colder. I heard some strange noises outside so I decided to take the kids inside; hoping whomever or whatever that was would pass us by quickly so we can hurry on. "Okay, we are going to go inside and take a quick rest," I whispered to them. I was trying my best to not to let them know that something wrong was going on.

We have only been walking for about 30 minutes since we were all the way in the back of the camp. I knew we couldn't go back inside any of the cabins. There were only a few safe spots that Shawn had set up and we already left one. It just wasn't a good idea anymore to stay at the back of the camp.

We had just made it to the front of the boy's cabins. And the only place over here that we could go inside is the mail room. We walked in and there was a pool of blood on the floor. Mail was scattered all over the place. We heard screaming just outside the mail room. I grabbed the kids and hid behind something. "Miss Rayna I'm scared." "I know, I know." All of a sudden the door burst opened. I had to cover Cody mouth just to keep him from screaming.

After the door was slammed it sounded as if someone was losing their balance. Things started to fall to the floor. I heard heavy breathing like someone was tired. The dropped to their knees. We sat so down low that we never got a look at their face. Until the door slammed shut again.

Whoever it was stood up and started backing up. "Please no. I beg you what do you want?" Whoever they were speaking to never said a thing. "There just kids. Please leave them alone don't hurt." Before he could get out the rest of his sentence he fell to the ground with a knife in his stomach.

I covered Cody's eyes while Cassie pressed her face into my body. I watched as the knife went in and out of his body like the killer was cutting steak. All these memories came flooding back to me. It was as if I was watching Danielle being murder all over again. Before he took his last breath Cody looked over at me. In that brief moment. I mouth that I was sorry and I could tell that he knew there wasn't anything that I could do.

Footsteps could be heard on the hardwood floors. Indicating that the killer was still in here. What could he possibly want? Does he think more people are in here? Did he see us come in here before he chased him in here to kill? All of these questions came flooding in but the only thing that I really wanted was for him to go away.

I looked to my right and saw, Jessie, one of the counselors lying there dead. I took a deep breath and bit my mouth to keep from screaming. I didn't want to alarm the kids or the killer. Please hurry up and leave so we can get out of here. The door slammed shut. Cassie's tried to get up but I grabbed her arm. "We cannot move just yet" I mouthed to them. "Be still and very quiet."

We sat there until I felt like it was safe enough for us to leave. I got out first to make sure it was safe for us to move on. If anything happens to me I know they could be safe if they stayed here until morning. So, it was better for me to go out and check.

I got up slowly and moved from under I froze. Seeing him lie there lifeless. It was sad and the fact that I couldn't do anything to help him. It made me feel weak all over again. I quickly went to the door to check to see if anything was out there. There were two more bodies. From the size of the bodies I knew they had to be kids. At that moment I knew I just had to get them out of this camp.

We heard screaming not too far from us. I just hope the killer isn't as close as the scream. I went back over to pull them up and hoping that they didn't look at the sight before them. But I knew they already had. "Come on guys we have to hurry." "Miss Rayna, what was that?" "I don't know and I don't want to find out. Come on we have to go now."

After we leave this mailroom the woods aren't too far off. We just have to make it past the old showers. We heard screams but I wasn't too sure where they were coming from. They didn't seem to be close so we kept on moving. We were almost to the woods. "Miss. Rayna I'm scared." "I know sweetheart but we are almost out of here. We just have to keep going."

Once we hit the edge of woods the screams seem to be getting closers. We started hearing rustling causing Cassie to gasps. We picked up our pace. I held onto Taylor's little hand as we rushed through the woods. There was a loud thud and I heard whimpers. "Miss Rayna." I turned around and saw Cassie on the ground reaching out to me. I went back and picked her up off the ground. I grabbed onto Cody's hand and took off running.

I'm pretty sure whoever that was close by heard us and we had to get out of the area fast. I tried to run as fast as I could but because I still had Carly and Marcus trailing after me I couldn't leave them behind. I was so happy to see the woods. I knew that we would have some type of cover from all the trees surrounding us since the rain let up a while ago.

We had barely made it into the woods and it was as if somebody was following us already. We weren't even close to the spot. I had to find a spot that we could hide quick. The noise seemed to be getting closers. I looked around for a place to hide. I picked Carly up and grabbed Marcus hand towards a bush.

Great Rayna back in the bush. This didn't work so great last time. As long as we stay hidden it should be fine. "Someone please help." We heard someone call out. "Please help me." They sounded as if they were out of breath. I wasn't taking a chance again. It's not my life that I have to worry about this time. If anything happened to this kids I would never forgive myself. I closed my eyes and softly said I'm sorry.

I remember this spot all too well. This is the place that basically saved my life. I would never forget this place. "Okay, now everybody get down there." they all crawled into the little whole. I picked up Carly and placed her tiny little self down below. I gather up some leaves the same as Shawn did years ago. I needed them to place over them. "Okay, now I'm going to put leaves on you guys so its harder for anyone to see you."

Once I placed the leaves over without it looking like they were placed there I started to push the log over. "Wait, Miss Rayna what about you?" "Yeah what are you doing?" "I'm sorry but I can't stay with you. I have to go back for Shawn." "Is he okay?" "I'm sure he's fine. I just have to go back. I promise I will be back for you guys. I need you all to be very quiet and still. Lala has the pack. There is enough food and water for you. Whatever you hear no matter what do not leave this spot. Promise me." "Promise." They all said.

I resumed pushing the log over the hole they were in. "Wait, Miss Rayna." "Yes." "Promise you will be alright." "I promise."

I rushed through the woods as fast as I could. I didn't care about anything else. My goal was to get to Shawn. He always sacrifices himself for others. Its always been his nature. I would find him no matter what. It was my time to protect him. That was my focus. My motivation. It was my turn.

Once I made it back to the camp I looked for Shawn right away. There were bodies all over the place. It was a sad sight but I was relieved that there were very few children.

"Where are the kids?" "Don't worry they're safe. What about the kids that were with you." "How do you think I got this wound." "Oh no." "They're fine as well no need to worry. I made them go ahead while I fought him off." "You found him? Well, what happened to him?" "I don't know I passed out. I guess he thought that I was dead and left me. I came in here because I need something to wrap up this wound."

I helped him patch up his wound. "Why are you staring at me like that?" "Because you know you shouldn't be here." "I came back for you." "I get that but." "But nothing I'm here now just be still." "I told you to get away so that you would be safe." "It's my time to protect you."

Looking at the moonlight reflecting off the lake. There stood the same abandon building. Cabin six nothing has changed. The ugly cabin looks like it did exactly 15 years ago. "So you think he's in there." "That's the only place he would go back to. Are you ready?" "Ready to finally get this over with." "Let's go." "Are you sure you are fine?" "Yeah, its time to end this."

We headed across the lake. That had to be the only place he could be. From what Shawn told me everyone on this side of the lake was dead. And those who weren't are somewhere safe.

We walked into the cabin six. There he stood cleaning his weapons. The door slammed shut making me jump. It didn't seem to phase him at all. "What are you doing here?" I heard Shawn say. I thought he was speaking to the killer until I heard his voice. "The same reason as you."

I turned around and was face to face with him. He was wounded. "Kirk." "Don't worry about me it's him we have to get." I napped my head back in the direction of the killer. You can see his knife gleaming in the moonlight. He walked closer to us. His movements were slow. If I remember correctly his movements were always slow. Like he was enjoying it.

He cocked his head to the side and looked at me. he had this look in his eyes as if he was remembering something. "Stay away from her," Shawn yelled. "Rayna get out of here. Take Kirk and leave now." "But." "I'm not going to say it again. Go!" While Shawn fought with the killer I helped Kirk up and went outside.

"We have to get you somewhere safe." "Don't worry about me. Just leave me. The only thing that matters is killing him. He must be stopped." The Killer came outside. "Shawn." Kirk looked in the direction I was looking at. He pushed me towards the woods. "Get out of here Rayna while you still can." "Kirk no you're hurt."

The killer started headed our way. "Just get out of here. I wasn't leaving. I came back to finally do something. Kirk went over to the killer and pulled something out of his pocket. It was too late the killer stabbed him in the stomach. He yelled out in pain and fell to the ground. "Kirk," I screamed. I looked around and found a branch.

He came over to me swinging his knife. I swing first and hit the knife out of his hand. I swung again and this time I hit him. I could win this. I swung again but this time he grabbed the branch and yanked me causing me to fall and hit my back on a rock. He picked up his knife and slashed my leg.

"I told you to stay away from her." "Shawn." Thank goodness he's okay. He came rushing over to the killer knocking him over. They were tossing back and forth. I picked up the knife he dropped. He was on top of Shawn. I jammed it in his back over and over. Shawn finally was able to push him off. He layed there lifeless. I really wanted to see his face.

Shawn came over to me. "Rayna its okay. It's okay. It's over." "Oh my gosh, Kirk." "Where is he?" "He was stabbed I don't Know if he's still alive." Just as we were about to walk over there. "Shawn watch out." But it was too late the killer hit him over the headed knocking him out.

"What do you want why are you doing this?" Again he spoke no words. But it didn't matter because he was going to be stopped. I wasn't willing to die out here and I wasn't going to let him kill Shawn. This was coming to an end once and for all.

He was going to burn. Somehow I had to lead him to the trap that Shawn set up. Provoking him to seem to be the best option. "You want me huh," I yelled. "Come and get me then. Come and kill me." He got up from where he was by Kirk and came after me. Just like I wanted.

I ran to where the old cave was. Shawn dug a hole there to trap him. The idea was to get him to fall inside and set it on fire. However, things never go as plan. I'm leaving a real-life horror story. I was bound to fall or get caught. Him cutting my leg just made that easier. It was throbing so bad I wasn't sure if I continue on.

Just as I looked back I stumbled on the ground. As I was about to get up I felt his presence over mines. this can't be the end. "This is the last time I'm saying this stay away from her." "Shawn." He came charging after him. The killer lifed his knife in the air. I hit him in the back of his knee with a stick causing him to drop the knife. Shawn tackled him to the ground. He picked up a rock and hit him over the head a few times.

The killer was still as if he was dead. "Come on let's go." He grabbed my hand and pulled me off the ground. We began running away in the direction of the cave again." "Shawn." "We have to keep moving we are almost there." Our only hope was to lead him to the hole. It was are a sure-fire way to make sure that he was dead this time.

We hid Once he reached us we pushed him down the hole. Shawn pulled out matches and lit the pit on fire. There was no way he was surviving this. Watching his body burn up in those flames was a sign of relief.  We did it, Danielle. Police sirens could be heard in the distance. It was over it was finally over.